THREE RIDE AGAIN

When surveyors working in Devil's Canyon are attacked and killed, it looks as if a full-scale Indian war is about to erupt. To make things worse, a murderer is at large in nearby Fort Bowie. If they are to stop the coming war and discover the identity of the mystery killer, three oddly matched blood brothers — a rancher, an Apache and a Zulu warrior — will have to forget their differences and ride shoulder to shoulder again.

STEVE HAYES AND
BEN BRIDGES

◆

THREE
RIDE AGAIN

Complete and Unabridged

LINFORD
Leicester

First published in Great Britain in 2013

First Linford Edition
published 2014

A catalogue record for this book is available
from the British Library.

ISBN 978–1–4448–2212–0

Published by
F. A. Thorpe (Publishing)
Anstey, Leicestershire

Set by Words & Graphics Ltd.
Anstey, Leicestershire
Printed and bound in Great Britain by
T. J. International Ltd., Padstow, Cornwall

This book is printed on acid-free paper

This is for Ed Martin,
who always keeps us covered.

1

Jim Lord read through his report one final time, then tucked it carefully into the manila folder before him. It pretty much confirmed everything the geologists had already said: that here in this wilderness white men called Devil's Canyon, lay a king's ransom in copper.

As he sat back, his camp chair creaked softly beneath him. That and the steady hiss of the Argand lamp swinging gently overhead were the only sounds in the peaked Sibley tent.

Lord stifled a yawn. It had been a long day and he was beat. But the outcome of the expedition had never really been in doubt. That Arizona contained a wealth in copper had been common knowledge ever since the closing days of the War, when a man named Clifton had made the first strike but never bothered to stake his claim because it lay in the middle of Indian country. A braver soul had subsequently staked it instead, and not long afterward, the Longfellow Copper Mining Company of Las Cruces, New Mexico, had turned the area into one of the territory's most prosperous mining communities.

Even then copper continued to be overlooked in favor of gold and silver. That was where the real money lay — or so it was believed. Few people seemed to realize the potential of *cuprum*, to give it its Latin name. It could be used in the production of shell cases, and to make copper sheeting and pipes. Combine with zinc it made brass. Combined with tin it made bronze. In liquid form, it preserved timber. It didn't corrode, so it could be used in shipbuilding, too. And both copper sulfate and copper oxide had proven medicinal properties.

Still, Lord's preliminary work was finished now. For him, the first stage of the job was over. But there was still plenty of hard toil ahead for his boss,

Cord Truman of the Truman Copper Consortium. There was a mine to dig, a smelter to construct, a rod mill to build, through which rock could be crushed and copper taken from it. Hard toil indeed . . . but well worth it, because the sedimentary samples the geologists had taken from the streambeds hereabouts, and which Lord himself had now had a chance to confirm firsthand, had all shown uncommonly high concentrations of copper. Lord reckoned the eventual yield could be as high as thirty percent — that was, about six hundred pounds of copper extracted from every two thousand pounds of rock mined.

From outside he heard the mournful quaver of a harmonica, and smiled. That would be their guide, Charlie Mason. Every night for the last three nights, the slightly built, walnut-faced old-timer had settled himself after their meager supper to play the harmonica for a while before turning in, and Lord had come to enjoy his impromptu performances.

For a second or so he struggled to identify the tune. Then . . . yes, he had it — *The Irish Mother's Lament*. And in that moment he realized just how much he was going to miss this rugged life when they returned to Fort Bowie in the morning. He'd only been out here for three days, it was true, but three days had been long enough for him to adapt to this simpler way of life.

Still, at least he'd be taking good news back with him. Truman, an abrasive cock bantam of a man, should be well pleased with his report. And with any luck the copper magnate might even start considering Lord himself in a more favorable light because of it.

Well, a man could hope.

As he had known they would, his thoughts quickly turned from Truman to Truman's daughter, Ann. With her pale oval face framed by flowing, shoulder-length hair as black as the fruit of a thorn, she was a vision. Indeed, her features — violet eyes, a

4

small, tip-tilted nose and full pink lips — were so perfectly in proportion that Lord found it almost impossible to believe that the toad-like Truman could have sired her.

But with thoughts of Ann came restlessness, too. Stupid, he knew, but abruptly he ached to be near her. If only Truman would drop his objections to their relationship — that Lord was too old for her, and a divorced man to boot — there was no good reason why they should ever be parted again.

Abruptly he rose and ducked out of the tent.

After the heat of the day the night had turned cool, and a persistent breeze whipped at the flames of the small campfire around which the others had gathered to drink coffee, smoke cigarettes and rest weary bones.

At thirty-seven, Lord was tall and muscular in his gray shirt and whipcord pants. Fair, collar-length hair just lightening to the color of dust topped his square, hardy face. As he came toward the fire and knelt to pour coffee, the others glanced up and nodded vague greetings.

'All finished?' asked Harry Ryan, his thin, bespectacled assistant.

'Uh-huh.'

'And it's as we thought?'

'It's *better*,' said Lord. 'If Truman plays his cards right, this canyon could well keep him in business 'til the turn of the century.'

Ryan grinned. Charlie Mason stopped playing his harmonica and called over: 'That mean we c'n expect some kinda bonus when we get back to Fort Bowie, Mr. Lord?'

The word made the other two men at the campfire sit up straighter. These were the two bodyguards Truman had insisted they take with them, rough-hewn, trail-wise men whose job it had been to keep a lookout for Apaches while Lord and Ryan carried out their survey. The taciturn beanpole with the shaggy black hair was Vern Barry, whose absence of teeth gave his face a sunken, caved-in look. Barry's companion, Red Taylor, was shorter and stockier, with a thick mane of fire-red hair and a crinkly beard to match.

'Now *there's* a notion,' allowed Taylor. 'What do you say, Mr. Lord? Would he go for that, you reckon? Your boss?'

'I wouldn't count on it,' Lord replied drily. 'But I'll be sure and mention it to him when we get back. You never know your luck.'

Out in the darkness, a coyote yipped mournfully at the moon. Lord found the sound oddly comforting, but Taylor shivered noticeably.

'Play somethin' cheerful, will you, Charlie?' he called suddenly.

Hairless but for a shaggy walrus moustache, Mason put the harmonica back to his lips and started playing *When Johnny Comes Marching Home*.

From the minute they'd arrived, Jim Lord had found Devil's Canyon a place of rare beauty. Though the land itself was scored through with deep canyons and the most tortured outcrops of rock he'd ever seen, it was also incredibly lush. There was plenty of timber — juniper, piñon pine, white oak and willow — and no shortage of cactus and chaparral. There was also plenty of water, plenty of game — and of course, plenty of copper.

Now he sat back and blew steam off his coffee. They had camped in a well-watered canyon choked with man-zanita, cholla and scrub live oak. At first the isolation of the place had troubled him, and he'd wondered if he'd ever get used to it. Then he'd realized just how *peaceful* everything was, and how that peace was infinitely preferable to the hustle and bustle of his normal, every-day life.

In one way he'd be sorry to return to civilization tomorrow . . . but in another he couldn't wait, because returning to Fort Bowie meant returning to Ann, and —

'What the hell's that?' muttered Vern Barry.

As Charlie Mason's harmonica fell silent, the beanpole climbed to his feet, his left hand brushing against the grips of his Police Colt.

They all looked out into the darkness. Nearby, one or two of their picketed horses stamped nervously.

'What's what?' asked Lord.

Barry jerked his chin. 'Up there, on yonder ridge.'

'I don't see nothin',' Mason said after a moment.

'Up there,' Barry said quietly. 'Looked like . . . '

They all saw it, then: a small, restless light at the very top of the canyon's jagged south ridge.

Lord thought, *What the hell . . . ?*

— a small, restless light that suddenly started growing larger, larger —

'*Apaches!*' bawled Barry, and a moment later the light — now identified as a flaming arrow — punched down into Lord's Sibley tent, immediately setting the dry canvas ablaze.

At the same moment the darkness to

the east exploded with a mixture of war cries, rifle fire and pounding hooves. As Lord spun that way, he saw a shadowy knot of Indians astride painted ponies surging out of the darkness toward him, firing their weapons into the sky.

The firelight showed him six or eight bronzed men in shirts and breech-clouts. Their faces were smeared with white-striped paint, their flying hair tied back with blood-red bands of cloth.

Lord stood frozen before them.

More flaming arrows started raining down from the canyon rim, finding targets in the other tents.

Then —

Vern Barry shoved Lord aside and hauled his Navy Colt just as the first of the Indians swept in. The lead rider — tall for an Apache, wearing a leather war-shirt and baggy white cotton breeches — immediately turned his charging horse toward him and used it to batter him aside. They collided with a hard smack of flesh and then Barry was slammed over onto his back.

Still staggering from the shove, Lord turned and ran for the burning Sibley tent, batted the flap aside, threw himself at the table and snatched up the manila folder containing his report.

Even as his fingers closed around it, he heard the raucous yell of an Apache right outside. The tent shivered as the guy ropes were plucked from the ground, and then the tent itself seemed to lurch sideways and collapse on top of him.

Lord dropped flat. For one agonizing instant the burning canvas scalded the forearms that he'd instinctively folded over his head; then the tent was gone, being dragged, still flaming, along the canyon floor, back in the direction from whence the Apaches had come.

A little crazy, he looked around. The campfire was now just a ragged line of coals glowing in the sand. Ryan and Mason were nowhere to be seen. In the center of the camp, Red Taylor had found his Peabody carbine and was sending lead after the departing Indians, but it was too late — they were already out of range, and the camp itself was wrecked.

At last Taylor stopped shooting, dropped to one knee and started loading fresh rounds into the Peabody. The night was beginning to stink of drifting smoke and burning canvas, and the horses were tugging frantically at their ropes, anxious to be elsewhere.

Vern Barry was on his hands and knees now, still dazed from his collision with the Apache pony and trying to gauge the extent of his injuries. By the light of the burning tents, all of which had been set ablaze by flaming arrows, Lord saw Ryan and Mason step out of tree-cover, both men looking shock-pale in the dancing light.

'Sonofabitch!' Mason breathed at last. He went over to where his discarded harmonica lay in the dust and picked it up, then set about trying to stamp out the nearest burning tent.

'Everyone okay?' asked Lord, his voice shaky. ' . . . Vern?'

'I'm fine,' growled the taciturn Barry.

Out in the darkness all that could be

seen now was the burning Sibley tent, still being dragged by the Apache who'd ripped it out of the ground. Then the darkness swallowed even that.

Lord cleared his throat. 'Will . . . will they be back?' he asked. 'We'd better — '

'You're safe enough now, I reckon,' said Taylor.

'You hope,' muttered Charlie Mason. 'If them Apaches'd meant business, we'd have had our hair lifted by now. What we just had was a *warnin'*.'

'Warning?' asked Ryan.

'Sure. They want us out of here.'

'You don't say,' said Charlie.

Around them, the night was cold and silent but for the spit and sputter of flames and the uneasy shifting of the frightened horses.

'Just as well we're leaving tomorrow, then,' said Lord.

'I'd prefer it if we left *now*,' said Ryan.

'You can do as you please,' grunted Taylor. 'Me, I'm stayin' right where I am 'til the sun comes up.'

Barry nodded, rubbing at his sore ribs. 'Only a fool moves through Indian country after dark. For now, we're better off right where we are.'

It was the most he'd said at any one time since they'd left Fort Bowie, and knowing he had a point, Charlie Mason looked up at the stars, gauging the time. 'Gonna be a *lo-o-ng, lo-o-ng* night, I'm thinkin',' he said.

That was when an arrow slashed out of nowhere and skewered him between the shoulders.

Before anyone could react, the Indians came galloping back out of the darkness, and it seemed to Lord that there were twice as many as there had been before.

Even as Mason crumpled face first to the ground, his harmonica slipping from his lifeless fingers, Harry Ryan twisted toward their attackers, then went rigid as one of the oncoming warriors thrust a feathered lance right through him.

14

The canyon exploded with gunfire and Jim Lord — unarmed, a *surveyor* for God's sake, not a *fighter* — did the only thing he could: he quickly threw himself among the nearby rocks, landed flat on his stomach and for an instant saw stars. Next second he was up on his elbows, wriggling as deep as he could go into the sea of silverbush beyond.

Back in what was left of their camp, Red Taylor turned, threw the stock of the reloaded carbine to his cheek and fired-levered-fired again. One of the Indians flipped backward off his horse and smashed hard against the ground. Then one of the Indians who had already galloped past turned his mount, came back at a dead run and slammed a flop-headed axe down on the crown of Red's hat. Taylor hunched up, grunted, fell sideways.

'*Red!*'

From deep in the brush, Lord saw Vern Barry shove his Colt to arm's length, fire a shot at the Indian who'd just killed his partner and miss. Behind

Barry, another Indian leapt down off his horse and sprinted forward. For an instant it was in Lord's mind to break cover and yell a warning, but —

But —

You coward! Damn you, you coward!

Instead the Indian crashed into Vern and Vern, taken completely by surprise, had no choice but to go down beneath him. They struggled for a while, with Barry twisting like an eel as he tried to unseat his opponent. Then the Indian raised one hand, firelight spilled off the blade of a knife, the knife came down —

Abruptly all movement in Vern Barry ceased.

Still yipping excitedly, the Indians milled around, the fires throwing their elongated shadows up across the seamed canyon walls. In the darkness, Lord now lay trembling, hating himself for his lack of guts, listening. In his mind he kept seeing Charlie Mason's eyes going wide as the arrow slammed into his back, Harry Ryan taking the lance through his body and crashing backwards, his hands gripping the feather-bedecked shaft as if perhaps he could pluck it free. He felt guilty that he alone had survived the attack, and that only because he'd run.

But what was he supposed to do? He wasn't a man of *action!* And even if he had been, he was unarmed.

The knowledge didn't help much.

Guttural shouts echoed through the night. At once he stopped breathing. Were they looking for him? Did the Indians know there had been five of them out here, and that they had only accounted for four?

Slowly, slowly he started to crawl deeper into the scrub. The serrated leaves were more like slivers of glass, opening painful hairline cuts on his face and arms with every inch he gained. Then a fresh burst of yapping came from the Indians behind him and he flattened, the manila folder crinkling beneath him, his fingers now clawing into the sand.

A few moments later the earth began to shake and he wondered what in hell was going to happen next. Then he heard the drum and pound of horse-hooves, and he realized that they had scattered the horses and were leaving.

He went slack with relief. Then, sweating and shaking, wanting to laugh one second and weep the next, he thrust his face into the sand, ashamed of himself, of his crippling fear. Even after silence fell over the canyon and the fires finally burned down to smoking embers, he lay there in an agony of self-hatred, hardly daring to breathe and certainly not daring to move.

And as the hours passed and it grew colder and colder, and out in the darkness the coyote finally started yipping again, he realized that Charlie Mason had been right.

It *was* a long, long night.

2

Jesse Glover set out for Fort Bowie a little after dawn, while the new day was still cold enough to fog a man's breath.

It had been a while since he'd last visited town, and having spent the past two months toiling more or less non-stop on his ranch, he'd come to realize that all work and no play had turned him into a mighty dull boy.

Even as he thought of the word *ranch*, however, he had to smile. All he had right now was a little frame cabin with a tarpaulin roof, a barn and a corral. You could hardly call it a ranch — yet. But for a man who'd spent most of his thirty years on the drift, it was the first real home he'd ever had, and one of these days it was going to be more than that; it was going to become his livelihood as well.

Tall and muscular, with a mane of

shaggy black hair poking out from beneath the brim of his low-crowned gray hat, Jesse had worked cattle practically his entire life, except for the nomadic childhood he'd spent travelling the west with his Indian Agent father. During those years, his father had gotten to know practically all the tribes, and along the way so had Jesse. Furthermore, old Jacob Glover had built a reputation for fairness and honesty among the Indians — traits the Indians had found rare in most whites.

It had been the hope of Ulysses S. Grant that the son would be as trusted as the father.

Knowing that Apache trouble was brewing in Arizona Territory, the Hero of Appomattox had requested Jesse go sort it out while there was still a chance for diplomacy. Jesse hadn't been too keen on the job, but when the man making the request also happened to be the President of the United States . . . well, there were some folks you just didn't say no to.

Against all the odds, Jesse had managed to do what Grant had asked of him, and to his surprise the job had changed his life in a way he had never foreseen.

The girl's name was Morning Star, and she was a White Mountain Apache. He guessed he'd fallen in love with her the minute he'd saved her from the *Comancheros* who'd killed her folks earlier that very same morning. And that's why he'd decided to stick around Fort Bowie when his work there was done. He'd figured to buy himself some land and go into the cattle business for himself, and when Morning Star saw what a fine, upstanding member of the community he'd become, maybe she'd feel about him the way he felt about her.

Still, even Jesse had to admit that was unlikely. He never had been able to figure out just what was going on behind those big, hazel-gold eyes of hers. Did she like him? Did she *love* him? Or did she just tolerate him?

It was anyone's guess.

It didn't help that he had a rival in the shape of an Apache Indian named Goyahkla, who also happened to be his blood brother. But the tie between them also worked to his advantage. For being the blood brother of Goyahkla, who was better known to the whites as Geronimo, gave him some measure of safety out there in what was still widely considered Apache country.

'Course, folks around Fort Bowie said he was crazy, trusting that blood-thirsty renegade to keep his word. With the Apaches forever cutting up rough, he was just asking for trouble. Sooner or later, they said, the Apaches would hit him and run off his stock, and that would be that, the end of his dream, if not of his life.

But not so long before, Jesse and Geronimo had stood shoulder to shoulder against a common enemy, and things like that had a way of forging bonds that could never be broken. They might never be *friends*, exactly, but for better or worse they *were* brothers, and when the chips were down that's what counted.

Besides, Jesse had found himself a parcel of land that was just perfect for his needs: thirty-six acres of grass-rich meadow dotted with wildflowers, ridge-lines spiked with piñon and juniper and deep, rain-fed arroyos. It was true that the only animals he could presently lay claim to were his golden sorrel, the pack-mule he now led by a tether and the elk, deer and antelope that wandered unchecked across his range, but Jesse was nothing if not an optimist. One of these days, he was going to have the biggest cattle ranch in this part of the territory.

One of these days . . .

He was still dreaming about his glowing future when Fort Bowie appeared on the horizon two hours later. It wasn't much of a place, even from a distance; little more than a wide stretch of dust between two facing rows of blocky, rough-hewn adobe buildings, at the far end of which sat the washed-out military post from which it took its name.

He tied up outside the mercantile, went inside with the pencil-written list he'd labored over the night before, and gave it to old Levi Cotton to fill. While the storekeeper was busy filling the order Jesse walked down to the barbershop, where he said he'd be wanting an all-over bath and a haircut before he headed for home.

The barber, a jockey-sized Italian with curly black hair that glistened with oil, stopped shearing his present customer and bobbed his head. '*Bagno*,' he said, '*si*, very good, Jess'. I boil thee water right now, you get it nice and hot, *va bene?*'

'Yeah, va benny.'

'You come back about t'irty minute.'

'I'll be here.'

Back on the street, he drew a breath and tried to decide on his next move. In the end his growling stomach made it for him. He hadn't eaten yet, and that was something else he'd been looking forward to: eating a meal that wasn't so much *cremated* as *cooked*.

He crossed the street and entered Singleton's Café. The place was packed, it being the breakfast hour, and he had to pause in the doorway while he searched for an empty table. There wasn't one. But off to his right he spotted Ethan Patch thoughtfully nursing a cup of coffee at a window table all by himself, and went over.

''Morning, Ethan. Stand some company?'

Fort Bowie's chief of scouts looked up in mild surprise. He was a tall, powerful-looking man in greasy buckskins, with a New Model Army Colt in a pouch high at his right hip. He was sixty or thereabouts, and his lined, saddle-leather face looked every day of it. He had cool blue eyes and a strawberry nose above a shaggy steerhorn moustache, and his long, unruly blond hair betrayed his Nordic ancestry.

'He'p yourself,' he invited, his voice a low, terse rumble. 'What brings you to town, stranger?'

Jesse pulled out a chair and sat across from him. 'Supplies.'

'How you doin' out there, anyway?'

'Tolerable. Place is startin' to look like a ranch, at last.'

'One of these days maybe I'll come out, give you a hand.'

'I could use it. There's only so much a man can do all by himself.'

Hazel Singleton, who waitressed at the café while her husband handled all the cooking, came over to take his order. Jesse settled on steak, eggs and coffee. When she'd gone, he said: 'How're things around here?'

'Quiet,' said Patch.

'*Too* quiet?'

'You know the Apaches. They might've gone to ground of late, but I doubt they've forgotten what happened at Camp Grant.'

Jesse's face darkened at the memory. About six months earlier, a mob of outraged citizens and Papago mercenaries from Tucson had shot, clubbed, raped and mutilated close to a hundred-fifty

Apaches in retaliation for an Apache raid in which six whites had died. The Apaches they'd killed had been mostly defenseless women and children.

''sides,' Patch continued, 'it could be that they're playin' a waitin' game.'

'How so?'

'Army's got its hands full with the Modocs in California and Oregon right now. Maybe they're just a-settin' back and lettin' them Modocs do all the killin' for 'em.' He studied Jesse shrewdly for a moment, then added casually: 'You'll have to ask Geronimo, next time he stops by.'

'I haven't seen much of Geronimo since we became blood brothers. I reckon he prefers it that way.'

'He sure has got a powerful hate for us whites,' Patch allowed. 'Must hurt like hell to have *your* blood in his veins.'

'I don't know why. It was Mexicans killed his wife and kids twenty-odd years ago, not us. And he sure as hell made *them* pay for it. But that's the trouble, I guess. Somewhere along the way hatred became a way of life for him, and *that* got into his blood, as well. He still doesn't trust anyone, and he's such a damn'-fool hot-head that he'd sooner strike first and deal with the consequences later — if at all.'

As he finished speaking he realized that Patch was no longer listening to him. The grizzled scout was staring out at Main Street, his jaw working thoughtfully. He was just about to ask Patch what was troubling him when Hazel delivered his order.

As he started eating Patch said: 'You got any idea of the time, Jess?'

Jesse took out his old Hunter and thumbed open the lid. 'Eight-thirty. You got to be someplace?'

'Nowhere but right here. But the eight o'clock stage is runnin' late.'

'From what I hear, the eight o'clock stage never gets into town 'til nine at the earliest. I don't know why they don't just call it the nine o'clock stage and be done with it.'

Patch nodded distractedly.

28

'You all right, Ethan?'

'What's that?'

'You seem a mite preoccupied.'

For one fleeting moment it was on Patch's tongue to deny the charge, but then he thought better of it and seemed almost to deflate. 'Truth to tell,' he sighed, 'I *am*.'

'Care to talk about it?'

Patch shrugged awkwardly. 'I'm s'posed to be meetin' my son off the stage,' he said in a rush. 'First time I seen him in almost eleven years.'

Jesse stopped chewing. He had no idea Patch had family, here or anywhere else. It must have shown in his face, because Patch offered up a sheepish grin.

'Oh, he ain't *blood*-kin. You might say I . . . adopted him when no one else wanted him.'

Jesse sliced through his steak. 'Sounds like you got a story to tell.'

'Not much of one. Just after the War started, Mangas Coloradas and Cochise decided to drive all us whites out of

Apache country. The idea caught on and pretty soon all the different bands came together in a loose kind of alliance — well, about as much of an alliance as the Apaches're ever likely to form. Geronimo was there, too, now that I come to think on it.

'Well, you know your history. Arizona was in chaos at the time, 'specially after the Confederates tried to annex it.'

'I heard about it,' said Jesse. 'They sent in the, ah . . . California Column, didn't they? To chase the rebels out again?'

'Yep. I was part of it: Fifth California Infantry under the command of Lieutenant-Colonel George Bowie. We marched right up the Butterfield Trail, figurin' to teach them Rebs a thing or two along the way. But before we found the Rebs we found the Apaches . . . and before we found the Apaches we found some of the folks they'd left behind 'em.'

His grizzled face turned bleak at the memory. 'One thing I'll say for the Apaches, Jess. They didn't play no favorites. Men, women, children — didn't matter who they were or what they did or how young or old they were. 'Long as they was white, they was fair game.

'Well, eventually we reached a place called El Rio, where they were still talkin' about how the Apaches'd hit a stage-coach station near Dragoon Springs six months earlier. 'Course, Butterfield had stopped runnin' coaches by then, what with the Apaches cuttin' up and the Confederates burnin' most of their stations to the ground. But it 'pears the folks who ran the Dragoon Springs station, family name of Redwood, they'd stayed on 'cause they didn't have no place else to go.

'The Redwoods and their daughters were killed. Locals went out and buried 'em, once the dust had settled. But there weren't no sign of the Redwoods' little boy, kid called Tyler. The locals figured the Apaches had taken him with them. Made sense. They sometimes take kids for trade, or to bolster their own numbers, especially if it's a boy-child.

'Well, about ten miles out of El Rio

the Apaches hit *my* outfit, too, and I guess that made it personal. We gave 'em hell and they ran, but not before a lot of good men died. Old Colonel Bowie was just about as mad as a hornet. He said we could go after 'em and finish the job if we was of a mind, and us with our fightin' blood up, we didn't need no second urgin'.

'So we went after 'em, tracked 'em up over the mountains just the other side of the Oro Valley and hit 'em in their camp a little after sunrise next mornin'.'

He paused, a cloud seeming to pass over him. 'Lot of women and children died that day too, though it wasn't our intention that they should. But in the heat of battle . . . well, let's just say it's not a thing I'm proud of. Toward the end of it, though, I seen this boy, runnin' for cover. Brown as a berry, he was, but his hair . . . it was fair.

'Didn't take much workin' out to realize he was white. I took after him, scooped him up, got him outta the line of fire. Kid tried to fight me every step of the way. But when I got him calmed down, I saw I was right. Fair hair, eyes just about as blue as a jay's wing . . . he was white, sure enough, though he'd become more'n a mite savage in the care of the Apaches.

'Turns out I'd found that missing boy, Tyler Redwood.

'After it was over, Bowie told me to take the boy back to El Rio, that he might have people there who'd take him in. But them folks in El Rio, they didn't care much for havin' a white boy turned feral in their midst. I couldn't abandon him, so I took him back to the column with me. Bowie, he was mad about it, an' he was right to be, for the column wasn't no place for that boy, especially after what he'd already been through. Didn't have much choice, though.

'In the time it took us to reach the next town, I grew partial to young Ty, and he took a shine to me, too. Turns out his pa — his *real* pa — was a hard man, and weren't no great loss to him. But I couldn't keep him with me, not where we was headed. So when we reached the next town I gave him over to the local marshal. I hated the thought that he'd be packed off to some orphanage back East, so I took it upon m'self to have him sent West instead, to a school I'd heard about in California, where they gave boys like him a good education and plenty of care.

'Just as well I did. We tangled with Cochise at Apache Pass just after that, then pushed on, only to find that the Confederates had let us march damn' near a thousand miles and then lit out ahead of us.'

'But you kept in touch with the boy,' said Jesse.

'He'd been torn away from his folks an' torn away from the Apaches. Didn't figure to let him get torn away from me, too. I ain't much for writin', but we kept in touch, after a fashion, an' over time I guess I became the closest thing he had to a pappy.'

'And *you?*'

'Like I say, I kind of adopted him, albeit unofficial-like. Now I'm his pa, and he's my boy, simple as that. Trouble is, I ain't seen him in years; got no real idea just what kind of a man he's grown into.'

This time it was Jesse's turn to be distracted. Catching movement through the café window, he suddenly sat a little straighter. 'Ethan,' he said, reaching for his coffee, 'I think you're just about to find out. Here comes the stage, right now.'

3

The stage came swaying along Main Street with a plume of dust chasing it in off the flats. Jesse and Patch watched it go by through the café window and come to a halt outside the Wells-Fargo office about midway down the street. Then Jesse looked over at Patch, who was still staring at the coach with something not unlike dread.

'Ethan,' he said softly.

'Huh? What was that?'

'Good luck,' said Jesse.

Patch looked at him. 'Why don't you come along with me,' he suggested. 'I can introduce you.'

It was, Jesse knew, the closest Patch would ever come to asking for moral support.

Setting some coins on the table, he said easily: 'Okay.'

The new arrivals were stepping down

off the coach and slapping dust from their clothes as the two men approached. Up on the coach roof the shotgun guard was already unstrapping luggage and tossing it down to the driver. As they drew nearer, a young man in a smart gray suit hopped down from the vehicle. He was about twenty, with a well-proportioned face, clear blue eyes and longish, carelessly brushed fair hair, over which he now stuck a muley hat. As he peered around, clearly searching for Patch, Jesse noticed an amulet hanging around his neck. It was shaped like an acorn, and the image of a bear, flanked by two bear prints, had been carved into it.

'Ty?'

The young man turned when Patch called his name, and Jesse watched as each evaluated the other. Tyler was clean-shaven, lightly tanned, with a straight nose and a firm jaw. He was about average in height but of slim, athletic build.

At last, self-consciously, Patch shoved out his callused right hand and Tyler took it. They looked into each other's eyes as they shook, and then Tyler's face split with a sudden, relieved grin and somehow the handshake was forgotten as, impulsively, he grabbed Patch and they slapped each other on the back.

'So . . . ' Patch said hesitantly, 'how was the, ah, journey, boy?'

'Long,' replied Tyler. 'But worth it, I hope. I've been wanting to come back to Arizona just about as long as I can recall.' He seemed to dry up then, and glanced questioningly at Jesse.

Taking the hint, Patch said: 'Want you to meet a friend of mine, Ty. This here's Jesse Glover. Good man to know. Jess . . . this here's my boy, Tyler Redwood.'

Jesse stuck out his hand. 'Pleased to meet you, Ty.'

The boy's grip was solid.

Tyler looked around, evaluating his surroundings. 'So this is Fort Bowie, huh?'

'What there is of it,' said Patch. 'I'll

show you round later, if you like. It won't take long. But first let's get you settled into a — '

'*Someone get the marshal out here, quick!*'

At once all heads turned in the direction of the yell.

A man dressed in range garb was leading his horse in off the flats. Slumped in the saddle was a second man, hatless and powdered with dust, his shoulders limp, his chin resting on his chest.

The sight could only mean one thing — trouble. And that being the case, Patch, as chief of scouts, immediately set off toward the newcomers, shoving through the townsfolk who were even now beginning to gather around them. Jess and Tyler exchanged a look, then went after him.

Even as Patch drew up beside the horse, the man astride it seemed to pour himself sideways out of the saddle. Patch, towering over everyone present, caught him easily, set him down on his feet, steadied him and then narrowed his eyes at the man who had led the horse in. 'It's Bob Sampson, isn't it?' he snapped. 'From the KD Connected? What's the story, Bob?'

Sampson was a short man with wide shoulders and bowed legs. 'Spotted him wanderin' out in the desert, Patch. Wasn't able to get much sense out of him, so I thought I'd better bring him straight in.'

'You got a name, feller?' asked Patch.

'*Jim!*'

Hard on the heels of her cry, a girl of about eighteen pushed urgently through the crowd, her expression becoming anguished when she finally saw the sorry state of the man she'd just identified. With a sob she almost threw herself at him, quickly snaking one arm around him and inspecting his injuries tearfully. She was beautiful, Jesse thought. Her pale face was framed by long black hair, her hourglass figure was encased in a well-tailored red velvet dress, and her eyes were an arresting shade of blue that didn't come along very often.

'Jim,' she said, choking with emotion, 'what happened?'

'Jim . . . ?' prodded Patch.

A short, pudgy man of middle age bulled his way into the center of the gathering to confront him. He had a round, corpulent face and a mouth that rose ever so slightly to one side, so that it seemed permanently fixed in a sneer. 'It's Jim Lord,' he said.

Patch glanced at him. 'And who're you?' he asked.

'Name's Cord Truman,' replied the fat man, his manner brisk and combative. He wore an expensively-cut suit of gunmetal gray, a bed-of-flowers vest and cravat held in place with a copper stickpin. 'I run the Truman Copper Consortium. That there's my daughter, Ann.'

'And who's this here feller to you?'

'He's a surveyor. He was doing some work for me.'

'What happened out there, Lord?' growled Patch.

Lord looked at him. His lips worked

41

for a few seconds, and then he croaked, 'Apaches.'

The word seemed to ripple though the onlookers.

'Th . . . they hit us, last night,' Lord continued. 'Fired our tents, r . . . ran off our horses, killed everyone.'

Truman's mouth sagged. '*Everyone?* Ryan — ?'

'Everyone,' Lord confirmed with feeling. 'Harry, old Charlie Mason, Berry and Taylor.'

A big, belligerent-looking man in the crowd cursed. '*Damn!* Charlie Mason was a friend o' mine!'

Again the crowd parted, this time to make way for a tall, skinny man in a well-worn black Stetson. The face beneath the curled hat brim was thin, fiftyish, with dark, narrowed eyes and a long nose above a drooping mustache the color of platinum; it belonged to Seth Keller, the marshal of Fort Bowie. 'Where did this happen, Lord?' he asked.

Before Lord could reply, Truman

said: 'That hardly matters right now! This man needs a doctor!'

'It matters to *me*,' said the marshal. 'Lord?'

'Devil's Canyon,' said Lord.

There followed a moment of silence.

Then someone said: 'That's what the Apaches call Gaan Canyon.'

It was Tyler.

Truman swung to face him. 'And what would *you* know about it?' he demanded.

'I know that Gaan Canyon's sacred land to the Apaches,' Tyler replied evenly. 'They've had a spiritual connection with that place for generations. Something else I know, too.'

'Oh?'

'That white men shouldn't be out there to begin with, much less surveying it for a copper mine!'

'That's not the way Major Calloway sees it,' Truman returned smugly.

Calloway. The name was like a red rag to Patch, and it had much the same effect on Jesse. Major Nicholas Calloway was the commanding officer at Fort Bowie, an embittered, overbearing Indian-hater who blamed everyone but himself for his continual lack of promotion. Grudgingly, Calloway had resigned himself to his position here at Bowie, but even being a big fish in a small pond hadn't done much to sweeten his disposition.

'I don't know who this man Calloway is,' said Tyler, 'but if he gave you permission to survey Gaan Canyon, he overstepped his authority.'

'Why? That land isn't protected by government treaty,' said Truman.

'Maybe not. But allowing people like you to go poking around out there can only have one consequence, Mr. Truman — provocation.'

Truman thrust his jaw forward belligerently. 'You're saying that's why the Apaches hit my people? Because we *provoked* them?'

'If the Apaches came here and burned down your churches, wouldn't that provoke *you?*'

'Who *are* you, anyway, boy?' Truman's dark brown eyes fell to the amulet around

Tyler's neck. 'You look and sound like an Indian-lover to me.'

There were a few muttered agreements to that.

'I'm just someone who believes in respecting the rights of others. You might have asked this Major Calloway of yours if you could go out to Gaan Canyon, but did you think to ask the Apaches?'

'I'm damned if I'd ask the Apaches for anything!' Truman bit back. 'And as for provocation, you're right, whoever you are — the minute those heathens attacked and killed the men in my employ, they pushed me a step too far, and I won't rest until Major Calloway clears them right out of this territory!'

Tyler smiled a brief, chilly smile. 'It never fails to amaze me how keen a man can be to make war when he isn't the one who has to do the fighting.'

Truman's fleshy face tightened with anger. But before he could respond the marshal said: 'All right, gents, calm down! That kind of talk ain't gettin' us anywhere! You there, Tom Haskell!' He indicated the aggrieved cowboy who'd been a friend of Charlie Mason. 'You and Sampson here take Mr. Lord down to the post infirmary. Mr. Truman, I'll want a full statement from him as soon as he's able to give one.'

'I'll see to it, marshal,' said Truman. But he couldn't resist giving Tyler one final glare. 'As for *you*,' he said, 'it might do you some good to think about the decent white men who died out there because of your stinking redsticks!'

His temper slipping, Tyler almost threw himself at the other man, but Jesse moved quickly, clamping his arms to his sides.

'Steady now, Ty.'

As the gathering began to break up, and a few departing locals threw black looks in Tyler's direction, Patch glowered at the young man and demanded: 'Just what the hell was *that* all about?'

Tyler colored. 'Like I said — I like to respect the other fellow, if I can.'

'Even if he's an Apache? Seems to me

you don't owe them a thing.'

Tyler ignored that, and shrugging himself out of Jesse's hold, said instead: 'Who's this Calloway character?'

'Runs Fort Bowie,' Patch replied shortly.

'Then I'd like to meet him.'

'Now, hold on a minute — '

'I mean it, Pa. If he lets Truman carry on surveying Gaan Canyon, you're going to have a full-scale war on your hands. You *know* you are.'

''course I know it,' Patch replied irritably. 'But you don't know Calloway. A full-scale war is likely just what that sanctimonious sonofabitch'd like right now. It'd be his time to shine.'

'And the men in his command?' asked Tyler. Without waiting for an answer he provided his own. 'It'll be their time to *die*, Pa. In big, bloody *batches*.'

4

It was coming on evening by the time the ranch came into sight. The sun had almost dropped behind the mountains and its dying light daubed the sky a million shades of ochre and vermillion. Now, as Jesse rode into the yard, freshly bathed, shaved and with his hair neatly trimmed, he reviewed the events of the day.

News of the Apache attack had spread quickly, as he'd known it would, and with it had come a mood of defiance and dread. The usual anti-Apache sentiments had immediately started doing the rounds, the usual questions about why the army hadn't done something about them red heathens long before this. Jesse, who'd heard it all before, of course, was amazed as always that no one could be bothered to see things from the Apaches' side.

Still, Patch had been right: Tyler hadn't done himself any favors by speaking up for them. When the crowd had finally broken up the looks cast his way had been little short of murderous. Undaunted, the boy had been all for going up to the fort and demanding an audience with Major Calloway, but as near as Jesse could see, Truman planned to get there first.

The abrasive little copper magnate had turned to leave, then halted when he realized his daughter was still fretting over Lord.

'Ann!'

The girl had looked at him, tears sparkling in her distinctive violet eyes. 'Father,' she'd said. 'Jim *needs* me.'

Truman's mouth narrowed. '*I* need you,' he replied. 'Jim'll get all the help he needs where these men are taking him.'

When she still made no move to join him, he snapped his fat fingers.

Lord squeezed her arm. 'Go on,' he said huskily. 'I'll be fine. Just shook up is all.'

She hesitated a moment more, then went to join her father. The girl kept a pace behind Truman as he set off toward the fort, her head lowered, her manner that of one well and truly beaten down. Only once did she dare glance back at Lord.

Then Tyler started speaking again. 'I'm sorry, Pa, but it's like I say. *Someone* has to speak out.'

'Even if it makes you about as welcome as a skunk at a picnic?'

Tyler squared his shoulders. 'Even then, I reckon.'

Patch considered that for a moment, then nodded. 'All right, Ty. You've had your say, an' what you said was dead right, but don't expect it to win you any friends. Now let's just hope this trouble blows over.'

'It won't, though, will it?' said Tyler.

Patch drew a long breath. 'Nope. Thing like this never does.'

Jesse bade them farewell and went to get his bath and haircut. When he stepped back out onto the street an hour later, he was just in time to see Calloway's adjutant, Lieutenant Alex Travers, leading a sixteen-man patrol out of the fort. Unless he was much mistaken, they were going to collect the bodies from Devil's Canyon.

After the soldiers had trotted past, Jesse stopped off in one of Fort Bowie's three saloons, where the other patrons, still grumbling about Tyler's outburst, quickly made it plain they considered him guilty by association. Taking the hint, Jesse finished his drink and went on his way, holding to Patch's forlorn hope that the Apache attack at Devil's Canyon would indeed blow over.

Now the day was closing and the sinking sun had created a jagged silhouette out of the mountains to the west. He swung down, deftly off-saddled the horse, unpacked the mule and turned them both out into the corral.

He was just about to pick up his supplies and lug them across to the cabin when he heard a soft scrape of sound behind him.

Immediately he twisted and dropped to a crouch, his single-action Colt appearing as if by some trickery in his hand. The hammer went *cli-cli-click* and a deep voice from the far corner of the cabin hurriedly called out: 'Don't shoot! I'm peaceable!'

Jesse straightened up and slid the Colt back into leather. 'Sam?' he called. 'That you?'

By way of answer, his unexpected visitor appeared around the corner of the cabin and strode toward him.

As a man, he was nothing short of magnificent. He stood well over six feet tall, and his broad shoulders tapered to a slim waist and lean flanks. Totally bald, with flake-gold eyes above raised cheekbones and a wide, unsmiling mouth above a strongly defined jaw, he wore an old pair of brown cavalry trousers tucked into scuffed preacher boots. His chest was bare, muscular, his skin a deep chocolate brown. Around each bicep he wore an armlet of white eagle feathers, and in his right hand he carried a short stabbing spear he called an *assegai*. At his waist hung a *bolas* — three rawhide thongs tied together at one end, with each of the free ends tied around a smooth, fist-sized rock. Jesse had seen his visitor use both weapons before, and knew how lethal they could be.

In these parts, he was known as Zulu Sam. Brought from Africa to America as a slave more than a decade earlier, he had escaped his southern masters just before the end of the War. Unable to return home by then, he had come west, eventually settling here in the Arizona Territory.

He was also blood brother to Jesse and Geronimo, for it had been these three who, some months earlier, had stood together against a crooked Indian Agent who had tried to frame the Apaches for his own crimes.

Now Sam held out one big hand and they clasped warmly. 'Dammit, Sam, you ought to know better than to come ghostin' up on a man like that.'

'I wasn't ghostin',' Sam replied, his accent a deep rumble that mixed American with Afrikaans. 'It's the only way I know how to move — quietly.'

'Well, you nearly got an extra hole where you really don't need one,' said Jesse, grinning. 'But I'm glad to see you, even if you did just scare me out of a year I can't afford to lose.'

Sam bent and picked up some of the supplies. 'I guessed you'd gone into town,' he said.

'Cupboards were gettin' awful bare,' Jesse replied. 'Figured it was about time I restocked.'

'You've heard the news, then,' said the Zulu.

'About what happened in Devil's Canyon, you mean?'

Sam nodded. 'I was there, Jess. I saw it all. That's why I come here now. To tell you.'

'What's it got to do with me?'

'Can't you guess?' asked Sam.

Jesse had just started across to the cabin. Now he pulled up sharp, for there could be only one answer to Sam's question.

'Geronimo?'

The Zulu nodded.

'Geronimo carried out that attack? Killed those — ' He broke off and swore. '*Damn* that fool Apache! He won't be satisfied 'til he starts a goddam — '

'There's more,' Sam said quietly.

Jesse regarded him closer, read something in his expression that he didn't like. They entered the cabin and Jesse dumped his supplies on the table and then got a lamp glowing. The single room was basic in the extreme: a table, two rawhide chairs, a low bed with a shuck mattress, a little Crosby & Co stove.

'Okay,' he said at last. 'Let's hear it.'

As Sam set his own share of the supplies down he said: 'I was over to Hackberry Creek when it happened, heard all the gunfire. Followed it as far as Rawhide Canyon, then had to lie low for a while, 'cause there were a couple of bowmen on the ridge. I recognized one of 'em, feller name of Blue Crow.'

'I know him,' said Jesse. 'He's pretty tight with Geronimo.'

'Anyway, I got there just in time to see Goyahkla and a bunch of like-minded hot-heads racin' out of the camp, trailin' a burning tent behind 'em.'

'And you're sure it *was* him?'

'Ain't no mistakin' Geronimo,' Sam said simply.

'Go on.'

'Knew better than to go down and help the whites. Shook up like they was, they'd have likely shot first and asked questions later. So I stayed up on the ridge just long enough to make sure they was okay. When I was sure they didn't need no help from me, I turned to go. That's when the Indians hit 'em again.'

His eyes met those of Jesse.

'Only this time,' he said quietly, 'it was a *different* bunch of Indians.'

'*What?*'

'There was at least twice as many this time,' said Sam. 'And they *weren't* Apaches.'

'Then who the hell were they?'

'Beats me. It all happened so fast, an' the light was pretty uncertain by then. But they played for keeps, Jess. Killed every man there, then chased off their horses.'

'They didn't kill *everyone*, Sam.'

'Huh?'

Jesse told him all about Jim Lord.

'Damn!' said Sam when his blood brother had finished. 'I'd have gone down there and given him a hand if I'd known. Way it looked to me was like they'd left everyone dead.'

'Never mind about that,' said Jesse. 'What do you make of it? This second bunch of Indians, I mean.'

'I don't know. But we'd better tell Geronimo, else just this once he's gonna take the blame for somethin' he *didn't* do.'

'I'd appreciate a few words with that damn' fool myself,' mused Jesse. 'Geronimo still stayin' in Cochise's stronghold?'

'Haven't heard any different.'

'All right. You eaten yet?'

'Not for a while.'

'Then set while I fix us some supper. We'll rest up here tonight and head up into the hills first thing tomorrow.'

'Sounds like a plan,' Sam replied. 'Just one thing.'

'What?'

'I've tasted your idea of food before, Jess. Tonight, *I'll* do the cookin'.'

5

It was only when Jesse headed for the barn next morning that he realized Sam had come in on foot the day before. Turning to the Zulu he said: 'You'll have to use my mule. Ain't no way you'll make it up to Cochise's camp under your own steam.'

But Sam only shook his head. 'I'll get a mount,' he said, and turning away, he stared out over the gray prairie.

Jesse watched him curiously. At last Sam tucked two fingers between his lips and loosed off a single, shrill whistle. The sound echoed across the plain and then vanished.

Jesse looked out into the dawn. Nothing stirred. He looked back at Sam. Sam just stood there, waiting. As if sensing Jesse's eyes on him, he said without turning around: 'Best saddle up, Jess. We' be movin' out shortly.'

Jesse nodded and turned back toward the stable. He managed three steps before he heard something behind him, and turned again.

A lone mustang was galloping in off the flats, its dark mane and tail bouncing with every powerful stride it took. Jesse grinned, knowing he shouldn't have been surprised even though he was. Still, it was hard to imagine that any man could share such a unique affinity with horses.

Now the mustang swept into the yard and came to a snorting, head-shaking halt before Sam, who reached up and cradled its muzzle in his big hands. Jesse looked at the horse. It was small and hardy, its coat a glistening light bay, the muscles beneath it bunching and twitching expectantly. The creature was wild as could be, and yet it showed no fear, wariness or aggression toward Sam, who grabbed a palmful of its mane and then swung easily up onto its back.

'We're waitin',' Sam called over.

Jesse nodded and went into the barn.

A few minutes later they were riding side by side across lonesome sage flats broken every so often by low gray hills, headed for the Dragoon Mountains and the cloud-scratching peak that served as their crown, Mount Glenn. There, somewhere among the very highest reaches, lay the stronghold of Cochise. The exact location was known only to a handful of white men, and that was how Cochise liked to keep it.

The morning wore on and mountains began to shove up out of the foothills around them. Once, drawing rein to give the animals a breather, Jesse cooled his saddle and sleeved sweat off his glistening face. Behind them now, the true extent of the land became apparent. The distant flats seemed to stretch into infinity, their immensity almost as awesome as their isolation.

He took a drink from his canteen and passed it to Sam. There was no doubt in either man that they'd already been spotted and their ascent reported back to the Chiricahua leader. For that reason Jesse took out a once-white kerchief and tied it to the barrel of his Winchester before remounting. Then he propped the rifle stock against one thigh, so that the kerchief could serve as a makeshift flag of truce.

They pushed on toward the timbered summit of Mount Glenn. The trail — though it could hardly be called such — was all dip and climb now. Brush grew dense in some places and virtually impenetrable in others. They climbed higher, only to find close-growing oaks and piñons forming yet another natural barrier.

Noon came and went. They passed precariously balanced towers of rock, crossed grass-rich meadows and walked their mounts through thin, echoing canyons, climbing all the while until, when they least expected it, they found the way ahead blocked by three Apaches.

The Indians seemed to appear out of nowhere. One carried a lance, the second a bow with an arrow ready-nocked, the third an old seven-shot Spencer carbine.

They stared at white man and black with expressions that betrayed nothing.

Jesse and Sam immediately reined down. Jesse's Apache was good but limited — he usually managed to communicate through sign and a little pidgin Spanish. Now he quickly wound his reins around the pommel and said, by way of greeting: '*Ya ta se.*' Then he tapped his chest. '*Ash.*'

It was the Apache word for friend.

The Apaches weren't sure about that. To them all the hated *pinda-lik-oyis* looked the same. But this particular *pinda-lik-oyi's* companion . . . there were not many like him, and they recognized him immediately.

'*Haskiiyii-Thii*,' said one of them. It was the name Geronimo had bestowed upon Sam. It translated as 'man-horse.'

Sam nodded. '*Haskiiyii-Thii*,' he repeated. 'We have come to see Goyahkla.'

The Apaches studied them for a few seconds more, then the one who had spoken nodded. He stamped forward on short, bowed legs and tore Jesse's

Winchester out of his hand. Then he gestured that Jesse should surrender his handgun, too. Reluctantly he did.

'*Hago*,' the Apache said, and then they all turned and began to jog tirelessly on up the trail. Sam and Jesse swapped a glance and then followed.

As they closed on the stronghold, Jesse felt his nerves begin to tingle. The Apaches tolerated him because of his father's reputation and the fact that he had stood with them when every other white man in the territory had been ready to wage war on them. The fact that he and Sam were Geronimo's blood brothers also played its part. But Jesse didn't kid himself. Aside from a little courtesy, the Apaches owed him nothing and they knew it. If he overstepped the bounds, even without meaning to, they would turn on him and then the Apache blood in his veins wouldn't count for squat.

And yet there was anticipation in him, too, because it was here that he'd see Morning Star again, if he was lucky, and that alone made the risk worthwhile.

The trail rose and then fell into a long, wide canyon shaded by large oaks. Jesse glanced up and saw lookouts perched here and there in high recesses carved out of the rugged rock walls. Further along the trail, beyond a wilderness of yucca, cactus and wind-eroded rocks, lay the stronghold itself.

It was a haphazard jumble of *wickiups* spaced out around occasional conical lodges built from wood chinked with dry mud. Smoke from a hundred cook-fires spiraled sluggishly skyward. They made the air smell like fresh-baked bread and boiled goose.

A stream ran through the village. Women washed clothes along its banks while their children kicked and splashed and laughed in the glittering shallows. A pool surrounded by rocks and yuccas lay further back, its surface still and oily black from this distance. Gaunt dogs padded here and there between dwellings, some yapping when they picked up the smell of white man, others chasing out to leap and frolic around the legs of their horses. Ignoring them, Jesse's eyes were everywhere now, searching for a glimpse of Morning Star. He didn't see her.

Men, women and children fell in behind them and followed them deeper into the *rancheria*. They studied the newcomers with open curiosity and more than a spark of concern, for the presence of a white man in their midst could mean little good.

At last he recognized a lodge situated at the very heart of the encampment, and the tall man standing before it, who was awaiting their arrival. This was the leader of the Chiricahuas — Cochise himself.

He wore a faded blue shirt and white cotton pants, and a red breechclout cloth tied around his middle. He was somewhere in his fifties, but the years had done little to diminish his powerful frame or the sharp, incisive light in his astute brown eyes. Strong and dignified, he had a large Roman nose, pronounced cheekbones, a grim set to his wide mouth.

Jesse and Sam reined down before him and an expectant silence immediately settled across the canyon. Even the children playing in the stream suddenly stopped their laughing and giggling, though none of them really knew why.

Finally Cochise spoke. '*Yaa' ta' sai,*' he said formally. It translated, roughly, as *welcome*. But Jesse had the distinct impression neither he nor Sam were especially welcome here.

'*A-key-yeh,*' Jesse replied solemnly.

'What is it that brings your steps to us, *Scan-To?*'

Scan-To. Jesse couldn't remember the last time he'd been called that. It was the name Morning Star had given him. It meant 'Sky-Eyes.'

'I have come to see Goyahkla,' Jesse replied. 'He and I have things to discuss.'

'What things?'

'They are between him and me.'

'That is not the Apache way,

Scan-To. We do not have secrets here.'

'It's not a secret, Cochise. It's just — '

'There is nothing between us that cannot be said openly!'

Jesse recognized the harsh snap of Geronimo's voice immediately, and turned just as the Apache pushed through the assembly and strode into the cleared area.

Geronimo glared up at him through dark, angry, close-set eyes. He was in his middle thirties — of an age with Sam — and his shoulder-length, center-parted hair was gleaming black. His name, *Goyahkla*, translated as 'One Who Yawns', but there was nothing sleepy about him now. He was wound as tight as a two-dollar watch, ever-belligerent and ready to fight at the slightest provocation.

Jesse looked down at him and said quietly: 'Are you *sure* about that, Goyahkla?'

Geronimo's jaw thrust forward. He was lean in his leather war shirt and loose cotton pants he tucked into knee-high moccasins. His headband was a sun-faded red, the belt at his waist decorated with silver conches. An ancient, long-barreled Manhattan Navy Revolver was stuffed behind the belt. A heavy-bladed knife sat in a bead-decorated sheath on his left hip.

'There is nothing *we* need to discuss in private,' he sneered.

'Then Cochise knows all about what happened in Gaan Canyon two nights ago?'

A muscle twitched in Geronimo's right cheek, but that was his only reaction. With a scowl Cochise said: 'Of what do you speak, *Scan-To?*'

Jesse looked from Geronimo to Cochise and back again. 'Why don't *you* tell him?'

'There is nothing to tell,' Geronimo said haughtily. 'Some whites set up camp in Gaan Canyon. They dug into the earth and took water from the streams and studied it. I thought they were miners and decided to scare them away before they could be joined by more of their kind.'

'And you did not think to ask my permission first?' asked Cochise.

'I did not see the need.'

'There is only one leader here, Goyahkla,' Cochise said menacingly.

'What would you have had me do?' countered Geronimo. 'Leave them alone, so that they might go back and fetch more of their kind to infest land which is ours?'

Cochise made no immediate reply, recognizing the truth in the other man's argument. 'What did you do to these white men?' he asked after a moment.

'We burned their tents.'

'And that was all?'

'All.'

'Then you are lucky. No great harm has been done. It will pass — I hope.'

'I'm not so sure, Cochise,' said Sam.

The Apache leader looked up at him.

'Goyahkla's right, as far as it goes,' Sam continued. 'He did exactly what he said he did to those whites. But after him and his friends had gone, another band came in and killed all but one of them and scattered their horses.'

Geronimo's expression slackened momentarily. 'What? You *lie!*'

'I was there,' Sam told him grimly. 'I *saw* it.'

'Who were these killers?' asked Cochise.

'I don't know,' said Sam. 'But accordin' to what Jesse here's already told me, the whites'll be comin' for *you* folks because of it. Unless . . . '

His deep voice trailed off.

'Speak, *Haskiiyii-Thii*,' said Cochise.

' . . . unless Goyahkla here goes into Fort Bowie and tells 'em what really happened,' Sam said flatly.

Geronimo reached up, grabbed Sam's forearm and wrenched him around. 'You are my brother,' he said. 'But more than that, you are my friend — and yet you ask me to cut my own throat?'

'Sam can tell the army what he saw,' said Jesse. 'But there's only one story that'll carry any weight with Major Calloway, and that's yours.'

'And you think he will believe me?'

'Why shouldn't he? Calloway might

71

not be the sharpest officer I've ever known, but even he knows the Apaches wouldn't give anyone else credit for a kill they made themselves.'

'*Calloway!*' Geronimo made the name sound more like an obscenity. 'He would have me jailed as soon as he saw me! He would take my word for nothing.'

'But your word, together with Sam's, might at least wake him up to the idea that we've got some renegades around here, stirrin' up trouble.'

'No,' said Geronimo. 'I will hunt these renegades, as you call them; I will track them and find them and kill them myself, and deliver their bodies to your fort. Then the whites will have their killers.'

'That won't satisfy them,' said Jesse. 'They do things differently, Goyahkla, you *know* they do. They have trials, they demand proof. There's no proof in a stack of bodies.'

'Then I tell you this, *Scan-To*. I will not go to the fort called Bowie. I will not willingly surrender myself to the whites.

Proof or no proof, they will hang me, because that is what they want to do.'

'Not even if going to Fort Bowie and puttin' your side of it means sparin' your people a whole lot of sufferin'?' asked Sam.

'*You* go. *You* tell them what you saw. If they believe you, we will talk again, and I will do whatever needs to be done. For now, I will handle this thing my own way.'

'Goyahkla!' snapped Cochise.

But Geronimo had already turned and was striding away, the assembled Apaches quickly forming a corridor for him.

Cochise sagged briefly, then recovered himself. 'There is truth in what he says,' he said quietly. 'This need for proof . . . the *pinda-lik-oyi* has no need of proof when it comes to the Apache. Only hatred counts for anything then. And with a man like this yellow-leg, this Calloway, hatred runs deep. Even for you, *Scan-To*.'

'I sure ain't his favorite person,' Jesse agreed. 'But there's more, Cochise.

Calloway's a major. By rights he should be a general by now, the years he's put in. But he's been passed over for promotion so many times that there's only one way left for him to get it now — by being the man who tamed the Apaches once an' for all.'

Cochise considered that. 'He *wants* war, then, this man?'

'He wants the promotion that will come with it — if he's successful. And he *will* be, Cochise. The army has guns and cannons and numbers. You can fight for a time. You might even score a victory, every now and then. But you know how it'll end up, same as me.'

'My instinct is to fight,' said the Chiricahua chief. 'But my heart tells me that many will die for no good reason. All right, *Scan-To*. You will speak with this Calloway, get him to see the truth of the matter.'

'And Goyahkla?' asked Sam.

'Leave Goyahkla to me,' Cochise said.

6

As soon as Cochise had disappeared back into his lodge, the Apache who'd taken Jesse's weapons from him handed them back, then wordlessly stamped away. Now that their audience with Cochise was over the assembly was breaking up, the people around them going back about their daily concerns. Jesse and Sam dismounted, anxious to head for Fort Bowie but knowing they would have to spell their horses — and themselves — for a while before starting the long journey down out of the mountains.

Jesse had just slid his Winchester back into its boot when Sam caught his eye across the dip of his saddle. Jesse looked over at his companion, who merely tilted his chin toward someone behind him. Scowling, Jesse turned — and froze.

Only one person was now left in the

cleared area before Cochise's lodge.

It was Morning Star.

She stood thirty feet away, with her arms down at her sides and her slender hands clenched into nervous fists. She wore a lime-green dress gathered in at the waist by a wide belt decorated with tacks and chain, and beaded leggings that ended in simple, unadorned moccasins.

Jesse felt the breath catch in his throat, for she'd lost nothing of her ability to entrance him. She was nineteen years old, and almost impossibly beautiful. Her coffee-colored skin was smooth as a bulrush, her face framed by raven-black hair that fell shining to the small of her back. Her large hazel-gold eyes were set above high cheekbones, her nose was small and appealingly snubbed, her lips full, almost defiant above a delicate, dimpled chin.

The lips now turned up at the corners in a smile that made his heart sing.

Jesse smiled back, foolishly. He was a lovesick puppy, and though he knew it, he could do nothing about it.

'Here,' said Sam, reaching for Jesse's reins. 'I'll go water the horses.'

Jesse barely heard him. He surrendered his reins without looking at his companion. Then he walked over to the girl, a familiar ache inside him reminding him how much he wanted her.

'Well,' he said when he was close enough. 'Fancy meetin' *you* here.' Inwardly he cringed, because it was such a dumb thing to say.

'You are well?' she said gently.

He nodded. 'Keepin' busy. You, uh . . . settlin' in here?'

'It is my home now,' she replied simply. 'And these are my people. I want for nothing. And I owe it to you.'

As they fell into step and started wandering aimlessly away from the clearing he said: 'How'd you figure that?'

'You saved me from one life, so that I could begin another.'

'I only did for you what I would've done for anyone.' He saw a spark of hurt in her eyes and added quickly:

''Course, of all the thousands of girls I've ever rescued, you're still the prettiest.' Then his good humor faded, and an old, nagging jealousy stirred within him. 'I bet Goyahkla feels the same way, huh?'

'He is a friend,' Morning Star reminded him.

'Is that all?'

'He would like to be more.'

'And would you *like* him to be more?'

'Is that any concern of yours?'

'I guess not.'

They walked on. Around them, women collected berries or edible plants, or gathered in small groups to play *stave*, a game of chance from which men were always excluded. Others busied themselves tanning hides or sewing clothes, while on the outskirts of town adolescent boys ran back and forth through the scrub, hunting for wood rats, prairie dogs or rabbits.

'The news you brought was not good,' she remarked. 'But then the news is never good between your people and mine.'

'Reckon not,' he replied. 'But maybe we'll . . . ah . . . change that, one of these days. You and me, I mean.'

She arched one delicate brow. 'Oh?'

'Just supposin',' he said with studied nonchalance, 'someone was to come along . . . I mean, just *supposin'* . . . an' this here feller offered to take you away from all this, set you up on a fine cattle ranch. You'd have a home of your own, somethin' more substantial than a *wickiup*, I mean . . . '

'I would not want anything more.'

'Not even if this feller was to, uh, say he had feelings for you? *Strong* ones?'

'I would need to have similar feelings for him,' she pointed out.

'You reckon you could have them for him? This feller?'

'I would not know that until I met him.'

'You already have,' said Jesse, stopping and turning her to face him. 'And you *know* it.'

She looked up at him, and now there was something else in her eyes — a depth of sorrow he had never previously suspected, and which shocked him. 'No,' she said after a moment, trying to choose her words carefully. 'You are white, I am Apache. We come from two different worlds.'

'I seem to recall you're only half-Apache. Your pa was a painter. Came from New Orleans.'

'Would you give up your white man's life and join me here?' she asked.

'Sure,' he said impulsively. 'If Cochise would let me. If it meant I could have you.'

'And you would not miss your old life?'

'Sure. Some.'

'Is that *truly* what you believe?'

'Yes,' he said. And then: 'No. Maybe in time.'

'I couldn't,' she told him. 'The life I know now is the life I have always known. Always known and always loved. I could no more adapt to your world than you could adapt to mine. And *you* know *that*.'

He stared into her face and saw for the first time a true indication of her feelings for him . . . and the impossibility of them.

Doggedly he said: 'We won't know 'til we try.'

'Won't we?'

He stepped back from her, feeling foolish now, and helpless. 'So I guess Goyahkla's the better prospect for you after all.'

'No,' she said. 'But one day, someone will be.'

'Just not me, huh?'

She shook her head.

'Well, that's straight enough, I guess.' Fighting hard to keep from showing his true feelings, he said: 'Guess I better go help Sam with the horses.'

'*Scan-To* . . . ' she said.

He turned back. 'What is it?'

Tears shone in her eyes as she said softly: '*Ka Dish Day*.'

He smiled fleetingly.

'*Ka Dish Day*,' he replied after a moment.

Until we meet again.

And before she could say another word, he turned and left her there, to watch him hurry away.

★   ★   ★

They made the journey down through the hills mostly in silence. Jesse had little desire to do anything but think about Morning Star and try to accept that all the fine plans he'd made to impress her were now going to come to naught. And Sam, guessing the direction his companion's thoughts had taken, left him alone with them and pondered his own problems instead, chief among how to get Major Calloway to accept his word that the Apaches weren't responsible for the deaths of the survey team.

Only when the sun began to set and they were forced to stop and make camp did Jesse finally speak. 'That damn' Geronimo,' he muttered.

Sam nodded. 'He's a trial, all right.

But facts are facts, Jess. He shows his face around Fort Bowie, he puts his head straight in a noose — 'specially if Calloway's got any say in it.'

'Then we'll just have to see what we can do between the two of us, won't we?'

They were up well before the sun next morning, only now Jesse had the distinct impression they were being followed. Maybe it was just imagination, but he'd learned to heed that itchy feeling at the back of his neck, so he made the rest of the journey with extra caution.

It was around mid-morning when his spread finally came into sight, and while still some distance out both men drew rein at what they saw waiting for them in the yard out front.

'Soldiers,' said Jesse.

'What do you reckon they want?'

'Don't know. Maybe they've found the renegades. Or maybe the sonsofbitches've struck again.'

They rode on. As they drew closer, they saw eight dusty troopers loafing around the yard, six new recruits and a couple of seasoned privates. A skinny sergeant with a permanent five o'clock shadow — Jesse knew him as a cheerless, unimaginative non-com named Emmett Farley — and a tall, red-haired lieutenant he'd never seen before were propping against the corral.

One of recruits spotted Jesse and Sam coming and called something to the lieutenant. The lieutenant turned, tugged at the hem of his blue sack coat and then marched forward to meet them, a sheathed saber knocking against his left leg with every pace he took. He was in his early twenties, as near as Jesse could judge, with freckled, sunburned skin and long side-whiskers. He had tucked a kerchief up under the back of his *kepi* to protect his neck from the sun.

As Jesse and Sam rode in, the lieutenant planted himself in their path and raised one gauntlet-covered hand to bring them to a halt. For a few seconds then he treated Jesse to an appraising glance.

He stared at Sam for considerably longer, having never seen his like before.

Turning back to Jesse he said: 'Mr. Glover, I presume?' His voice held the broad, nasal tones of the East.

Jesse nodded.

'I am Lieutenant Miles Madsen. We've been waiting for you.'

There was a hint of rebuke in the statement that immediately made Jesse's hackles rise.

'Well,' he replied, 'I'm right sorry about that, Lieutenant Miles Madsen. But I had business elsewhere.'

'May I ask *what* business, Mr. Glover?'

Jesse smiled coolly at that. 'Sure you can *ask*,' he said easily.

Madsen drew air in through his long nose. 'We have need of your services, sir,' he said stiffly. 'I require a scout to — '

'Lieutenant,' said Jesse, 'before you go any further, I'm not for hire. I've already got a job — right here.'

'Nevertheless, I — '

'You're not listening to me,' said

Jesse, his voice hardening a notch. 'I've just come in from a long, hard ride, mister. Right now all I want is to see to my horse and then get in out of this heat. After that I figure to boil some coffee, kick off my boots and rest my weary bones 'til suppertime. Now, I'm sorry you came all the way out here thinking you could hire me to scout for you, but I'm not a scout an' never have been, and like I just said, I got other plans.'

'They told me at Fort Bowie that you were the best man for the job at hand.'

'Then they told you false, lieutenant. I can track, sure, but there's plenty can do it better than me, not the least of 'em being Ethan Patch. Use *him*.'

'We can't,' said Madsen. 'Patch is one of the men we're trying to find.'

Not expecting that, Jesse gave him a sharp look. 'What's happened to him?' he asked.

Madsen countered with a question of his own. 'Do you know a man named Cord Truman?'

'I wouldn't say as I know him. He runs that copper mining company that sent the surveyors into Devil's Canyon.'

'He's dead,' Madsen said bluntly. 'He was murdered last night.'

'Where does Ethan Patch fit into it?'

'The killer was his adopted son,' said Madsen grimly. 'A man called Tyler Redwood.'

7

Jesse and Sam exchanged a look. Then: 'You know that for a fact?'

'Oh, he did it, all right,' said Madsen. 'He was seen by the hotel clerk arriving to see Truman, and then leaving again at a run not two minutes later.'

'That doesn't prove a damn' thing.'

'Not by itself, no. But Mr. Truman was found clutching some kind of amulet the boy had been seen wearing around his neck. And this Redwood boy took a horse from Gravey's Barn and left town, headed northeast. Not the sort of actions you'd normally associate with an innocent man, as I'm sure you'll agree.'

'And Patch . . . ?'

'When the news of the crime reached Patch, he went after his son. I have been tasked with finding this boy Redwood, and Patch himself.'

'Patch didn't come back?'

'No, sir, he did *not*.'

Jesse's immediate impulse was to help. He didn't know Tyler well enough to say one way or the other if he could kill a man, but Patch was a friend, and if anything happened to him —

But Patch could take care of himself. It would be child's play for him to run a tenderfoot like Tyler to ground. Still, the fact that he hadn't already brought the boy in could only mean one of two things: either Patch had run into trouble and needed help . . . or he'd decided to throw in with his boy.

'I'm sorry, lieutenant,' he said after a moment. 'I'd sooner not get involved.'

'I was told Patch was a friend of yours.'

'He is. That's why I'd sooner sit this one out.'

Madsen's lip curled. ''All that is necessary for the triumph of evil is that good men do nothing,'' he quoted.

'I'm just mindin' my own business, Madsen. There's a difference. Now, if you're finished, I reckon you can take your men and get the hell off my property.'

Madsen bit back whatever he was going to say and nodded. 'It'll be a pleasure, sir. I'm new to the West, as you can doubtless tell, and Fort Bowie is my first posting. They spoke highly of you at the fort . . . I can't say as I understand why.'

Jesse heeled his horse forward and the lieutenant had to step aside hurriedly. Sam followed him across the yard, watched by the curious troopers, then swung down and watched as Madsen barked orders to Sergeant Farley. Farley relayed them to the men. Horses were caught up, girths tightened, the men mounted up and, with Madsen at their head, they rode out in a short, dust-raising column of twos with nary a backward glance.

When they were gone, Jesse said: 'Step inside, Sam. Figure we'll get a bite to eat and then go find Patch.'

Sam grinned with relief. 'Glad to

hear you say that, brother. You had me wonderin' for a while, there.'

'If Ethan or his boy's in trouble, they'll need *friends* right now, not some tinhorn soldier out to arrest 'em.'

'Sure. But what can we do?'

'We won't know that 'til we find 'em and get the truth of it.'

'Fair enough,' said Sam. 'I'll take care o' the horses while you go fix up some chow, so long as you promise not to char the life out of it — '

He stopped abruptly.

Jesse said: 'What is it?'

'Rider comin' in.'

Recalling the feeling he'd had up in the high country, Jesse looked toward the flats beyond the yard. 'I don't see anyone.'

'He's out there,' said Sam, unshakable in his certainty. 'And he's headed this way.'

Jesse walked across the yard, mystified as always by the heightened senses Sam seemed to possess. Maybe he'd been born with them. Or maybe he'd somehow absorbed them from the wild horses among whom he lived. Either way, it was a puzzle.

Before he went into the cabin, he made one final search of the flats, but still saw nothing.

He was just rustling up some food when Sam came inside and said quietly: 'He's here.'

'Who's here?'

Even before he finished speaking he heard the sound of a shoeless horse entering the yard and strode to the door. He got there just as Geronimo swung down from a wiry pinto that was mostly white, with light bay haunches.

'*You!*' he said. 'Didn't figure we'd see you around here any time soon.'

Geronimo glowered at him. 'I will go with you to the yellow-legs at Fort Bowie,' he said. His tone said he'd sooner stick pins in his eyes.

Jesse studied him without appearing to. He couldn't say for sure what had happened after he and Sam had left the stronghold, but it was easy enough to guess. Cochise had sought out

Geronimo and told him what he must do. Geronimo wouldn't have liked it — he had a hard time taking orders from any man — but he knew better than to buck Cochise. And so he was here now, with the intention of accompanying them to Fort Bowie, and hating the taste of humble pie something fierce.

Jesse said nothing of his thoughts. There was no call to humiliate Geronimo further. What he said instead was: 'That'll have to wait. Somethin' else has come up.'

'What?'

Jesse told him.

'That is what the yellow-legs were doing here, then?' Geronimo muttered after he'd finished. 'They wanted you to track Patch for them.'

'Yup. But the way we figure it, we'd sooner us find Patch before the army does, and hear his side of the story.'

Geronimo nodded, for Patch was one of the very few men for whom he held any great respect. 'I will help,' he said simply.

Jesse nodded. 'All right. Accordin' to that prissy lieutenant, Tyler was ridin' northeast when he left town. Course, he could've gone in any direction after that, but we won't know for sure 'til we pick up his or Ethan's tracks, and at least northeast of Fort Bowie gives us a place to start. You're about the best tracker I know, Goyahkla, and Sam, I reckon you can just about track a flea across glass. So you two split up and see what you can find.'

'And you?' asked Geronimo.

'I'll ride into town itself,' Jesse replied. 'Have a look around. See what I can learn about this here Truman character, and exactly what happened.'

* * *

Jesse had no sure idea what he expected to find in Fort Bowie, but he had a bad feeling he wasn't going to like it.

As soon as he entered town, the locals started giving him the evil eye. No one had forgotten about his tenuous connection with Tyler, then, he told himself grimly. A man named Sorensen, who ran the meat market, came out onto his boardwalk to watch him pass, then crossed the street in a rush, blood-stained apron flapping around his bony knees.

Jesse wondered where the man was headed and whether or not it had anything to do with him.

Trying his best to ignore the looks he continued to receive, he tied up outside the marshal's office, which was a squat, whitewashed adobe building with small, barred windows, and tried the strap-steel door. It was locked. He looked up and down Main. It was already heading for noon — it could be Marshal Keller was having an early lunch down at Singleton's.

Before Jesse could go in search of him, however, someone called his name from the other side of the street.

He turned. A big, sturdy man in his late forties was crossing the street toward him with two other men in tow.

He had a sun-reddened face and pocked skin, a sour twist to his mouth and crooked teeth showing in a grimace. The two men with him were also cowhands, judging from the way they dressed, younger by ten or fifteen years.

Jesse didn't think he knew them until he took a closer look at the man with the crooked teeth, who'd called his name. Then he recognized him as Tom Haskell, the man who'd said he was a friend of old Charlie Mason, back when that KD Connected hand had first brought Jim Lord in off the desert.

Haskell came to a halt in front of him, his two companions stopping just a pace behind. Way beyond them he saw Sorensen, now back outside his meat market, watching them nervously. That's where the sonofabitch had gone then — to fetch Haskell.

'You got a nerve, showing your face here, Glover,' said Haskell. He had a slow, rumbling voice like gravel. 'But I'm mighty glad to see you.'

Jesse frowned. 'Are you, now?' he said guardedly.

'Yeah — 'cause now you can tell us where it is we can find that Indian-lovin' murderer you're so friendly with.'

Jesse sighed softly. 'You got the wrong man, fellers. In the first place, you don't know for sure that he's a killer. In the second, I don't know where he is and there's no good reason why I should, since I only met him for the first an' only time two days ago. And in the third place, suppose I *did* know where he was? What would you do about it? Find him and hang him . . . or bring him in for a fair trial?'

'*That*,' said Haskell, 'is none of your beeswax. But could you blame us if we *did* hang him? Lot of decent folks hereabouts have had our fill of the Apaches. They killed four good men out there in Devil's Canyon, one of 'em a friend of mine. Four men who was only doin' their jobs — '

' — and just so happened to be traipsin' all over the Apaches' sacred

97

ground to do it.'

' — and then your Indian-lovin' buddy goes and kills this here Truman feller, who was gonna bring jobs an' trade to this part of the territory, both of which it could use. So yeah, we want the sonofabitch who killed him.'

'Well, I don't know where he is.'

'And you expect us to take your word for that?'

Jesse's eyes hardened fractionally. 'You'd *better*.'

Haskell tilted his head to one side. 'An' if I choose not to? What then?'

'Then you an' me got a problem,' said Jesse. 'Now, just leave it. I know feelin's runnin' high. Didn't expect any different. But if you've got any sense, you'll set back and let the law or the army handle it. You'll see justice served eventually.'

'I don't care about that,' said Haskell. 'Like I say, Charlie Mason was a friend of mine. Good man. Shouldn't ought to've died the way he did.'

'None of them should,' said Jesse. He

fixed Haskell eye to eye. 'All right — you've had your say. Now I'll have mine. Get out of my road, Haskell. I got business elsewhere.'

'You ain't got no business in Fort Bowie,' Haskell breathed. 'Not until you step on over to the right side.'

'*Your* side?'

'Where's he hidin', Glover?' asked the man to Haskell's left. He was Mexican, with dark skin and a black mustache shaped like an upside-down horseshoe.

'You're not listenin',' said Jesse. 'I don't *know*.'

'I say you're lyin',' said Haskell. 'You're in it with him. You, Patch, him.'

Tired of it now, Jesse said bluntly: 'Are you clearin' my path or not?'

Haskell said: 'Not.'

And went for his gun.

Jesse knew a fractional moment of disbelief. Was the man actually so consumed by hatred that he was prepared to start a shooting match over it?

But even as he asked himself the question, Jesse flung himself at Haskell, crowding him, giving him no room to complete his draw. He swatted Haskell's hand away from his Colt, and slammed a punch at Haskell's jaw that sent him spilling backward into his two cronies.

'That's enough!' Jesse snapped. 'This is nothing to get killed over — or to risk shootin' some other poor soul for!'

But Haskell didn't see it that way. As his friends boosted him back on his feet he threw himself at Jesse, and Jesse had no choice but to defend himself.

Haskell came in like a crazy man. There was no science to him, just one swinging blow after another, a whole cloudburst of them, and Jesse had no choice but to step back, blocking as many as he could, his guard tight against his sides, his head sunk into his shoulders.

Suddenly his heels came up against the boardwalk and he lost balance. He fell back and Haskell followed him down. At once Haskell's two companions, the Mexican and a skinny cowboy with a wall eye, began yelling for Haskell to finish him.

The two combatants rolled over, grappling for control. Teeth clenched, Jesse heaved and Haskell fell aside, rolled some more and almost leapt back to his feet. He was big and mean and fired up, and Jesse didn't think he could stand much chance against him if he kept fighting the way he was.

He needed to end it quick.

He slammed a fist into Haskell's midriff. He saw the man's craggy face go slack, his ice-blue eyes bulge, and then crashed his fist against the man's jaw, snapping his head sideways, rocking him back on his heels.

Haskell stumbled sideways, spilled into the dust, and Jesse told himself, *It's over*.

But it wasn't.

Haskell's two friends, no longer content just to cheer their man on, immediately threw themselves into the fray and all at once Jesse was fighting again.

He caught a punch on the cheekbone. Instantly his face went numb. Wall Eye came at him from behind, grabbed his arms and jerked them around to his back. The Mexican came at him from the front, hit him hard in the stomach. Stars burst in his head and he felt like throwing up.

The Mexican drew back his fist, intending to give him some more of the same, but before the blow could land someone charged him from the left. He smashed into him and the two of them went down in a heap, with the newcomer on top.

Jesse felt the grip on his arms slacken, and quickly, mercilessly brought his head back into Wall Eye's face. Wall Eye howled, released his hold, and Jesse whirled toward him, saw that blood had squirted from his broken nose to stain the lower half of his ugly face red.

Grimacing, he let go a right hook and that lifted Wall Eye onto his toes. The man stiffened, and then his legs jellified and he collapsed.

Jesse twisted again, this time figuring to help his Good Samaritan, but even as he did so Haskell roared back into the fight, slamming him across the nape with a two-handed blow that sent him sprawling out into the street.

He stumbled, came up hard against something that grunted in surprise — a horse. The animal shied away from him and doggedly he turned to meet his enemy yet again, until the click of a handgun coming to full cock directly at the back of his head froze him in his tracks.

'That's *enough*, Mr. Glover!' snapped a voice behind and above him — the voice of the horse's rider. 'One more move and I'll shoot you where you *stand!*'

Everything stopped: Haskell, crouching to meet the attack; Wall Eye, cupping his bloody nose just behind him; and the Mexican, who'd just been knocked stupid by the man who had come to Jesse's aid . . . Jim Lord.

And in that sudden stillness Jesse finally recognized the voice behind him. He turned slowly, craning his neck to look up into the face of Major Nicholas Calloway, commander of Fort Bowie.

8

Calloway's sour disposition showed clearly in his pasty face. He was a heavy-set man in his early forties, with dark, hostile eyes and, beneath a bristling mustache with carefully waxed ends, a mouth that seemed set in a permanent grimace. It was quite possible that once he'd been a dashing young officer with a bright future ahead of him, but there was no evidence to suggest it now. Calloway was out of condition and looked it. He was a man who'd come into the service with high ambitions and been overlooked time and again in favor of younger, cleverer, braver men. He was an exceptional administrator, but the sifting of paperwork had never led to promotion or recognition or the acquisition of medals, and it never would.

He hated Jesse because President Grant had sent him in to do the very thing Calloway himself had been unable to do — broker a peace of sorts with the Apaches — and he hated Jesse even more because Jesse had done it and made it look easy.

'Take that gun out of my face,' Jesse managed between heaving breaths.

Calloway looked down at him. 'I always did say you were a troublemaker, Glover.'

'And I always did say you were a damn' blow-hard,' Jesse returned. 'Now take that gun out of my face or I'll do it for you.'

Calloway looked into his face, his eyes, and saw something dark and determined there that he didn't like. He put the gun up, set the trigger down, returned the big Cavalry Colt to its covered holster even as Marshal Keller came trotting up, a faint trace of egg yolk still clinging to his unclipped moustache.

'What's going on here?' he demanded.

'I want you to arrest this man for disturbing the peace,' said Calloway.

Keller looked at the carnage. 'If I arrest one, I have to arrest 'em all,' he said. Then: 'What happened here, Jesse?'

Before he could reply, Haskell said: 'He knows where that Indian-lovin' killer's holed up, and he ain't sayin'!'

Keller said: 'Do you, Jess?'

''course not.'

'That's good enough for me.'

Astride his horse, Calloway bridled. 'Now see here, Marshal! This man may have a point. If there's any chance that we can obtain the whereabouts of — '

'Jesse Glover's word's good enough for me,' said Keller. 'Always has been, always will be. But I tell you what I'll do, Major. I'll take him in for questioning, all right? Turns out he's lyin', you'll be the first to hear about it. But I wouldn't hold my breath waitin', was I you.'

He quickly turned his back on Calloway, effectively dismissing him with the gesture. 'Haskell! You and your friends go get yourselves cleaned up. I've heard about all the rumors you been spreadin' about Ethan Patch's boy. Keep it up and I'll post you out of town.'

'You can't do that,' growled Haskell.

'Can, and will,' Keller replied evenly. 'Incitement to riot. Now get the hell out of my sight.' He fixed Jesse with a look. 'Step into my office, boy.'

As the crowd began to break up, Jesse went over to Lord, who was dabbing a split lip with the back of one hand. The surveyor looked considerably better than the last time Jesse had seen him, but there was still something haunted in his gray eyes. Jesse noted that he was wearing a black armband, in memory of his murdered boss.

'Thanks for buying into that little donnybrook,' he said, offering his hand.

Lord took it without hesitation. 'Glad I could do something to help. I never did care much for bullies.'

'And you don't listen to idle gossip, either,' said Jesse. 'That's something else in your favor.'

'I understand that feelings are running high, but I won't hold one man responsible for another man's crime. Besides . . . '

'What?'

'Oh, nothing,' Lord said dismissively.

'Well, I appreciate it. Name's Jesse Glover. Like to buy you a drink, maybe later on.'

'Sure. I'm staying over at the Harper House. Look me up when you get through with the marshal.'

'I'll do that.'

Keller had unlocked the office door by then and as Jesse went inside the lawman was just setting a fresh pot of coffee on the stove.

'Sorry I interrupted your breakfast, Seth.'

'How's that again?'

'You've still got most of it trapped in your mustache.'

The lawman dragged out a kerchief and wiped his mouth. 'You look a mess,' he said bluntly. 'Go out back and clean yourself up.'

'Obliged.'

Behind a threadbare curtain sat a bunk and a chamber set for the times when Keller had to stay overnight in the jail. Jesse spilled cold water into the bowl and gingerly dabbed at his cuts and bruises.

'What brings you back to town so soon, anyway?' called Keller. 'You might'a known you'd be as welcome as a bullet around here after what happened last night.'

'What *did* happen, anyway?'

'Near as I can figure, young Redwood went up to see Cord Truman at his hotel.'

'The Harper House?'

'No, the Reagan place.'

'Go on.'

'Well, I guess he was still mad at Truman for sending his men out to Devil's Canyon and to hell with the Apaches. Near as I could figure it, there was a fight and Truman got his skull caved in.'

'But how do you know it was Tyler who did it?'

'Hotel clerk saw him come in an' then leave not two minutes later. Said the kid was white as a sheet and in a powerful hurry.'

Jesse came back into the office,

drying himself on an old towel. 'That's not enough to hang him.'

'No. But the fact that he stole a horse and lit out kind of condemns him, don't it? That an' the amulet we found in the deceased's hand.'

'I guess.'

'Anyway, we got the testimony of Truman's daughter. She caught Redwood in the act, so to speak, started screamin' an' scared him off.'

'Patch took off after him,' said Jesse, accepting a cup of coffee from the lawman.

Keller bobbed his head. 'Just as soon as he got the news. Haven't seen him since. But Patch can take care of hisself. If he hasn't brought that boy in, it's 'cause he knows what'll happen when he does.'

'You *really* think folks hereabouts might dispense a little hang-rope justice?'

'Truman made a lot of big promises when he first came to town, built up a lot hopes. It only takes a couple hot-heads like Tom Haskell and I might just have to call in the army.'

'So long as they don't send you Lieutenant Madsen.'

Keller blew steam off his coffee. 'You've met him, have you?'

'Him and a million just like him,' Jesse replied tiredly. 'A by-the-book soldier who'll never realize 'til it's too late that the Apaches didn't read the same book.' He drained his cup and set it down on the lawman's desk. 'Well, let's just hope this thing sorts itself out before it comes to that.'

'Amen, brother,' said Keller.

★ ★ ★

Jesse stepped back out onto the street. The day was as hot as a skillet. He weighed his next action for a few moments, then turned his steps toward the Reagan Hotel.

The carpeted lobby was deserted but for the clerk, a tall, trim man in a buttoned black vest over a white shirt, who was leaning with his elbows on the counter, reading a book. He looked up when Jesse came inside, and pushed himself erect. He had the pallor of one who spends most of his days indoors, a bald head, and round, wire-framed spectacles.

'Help you?' he enquired.

Jesse braced his hands on the edge of the counter. 'Wonder if I could ask you a few questions about the murder.'

The clerk rolled his eyes. 'I'm all done talking about that!' he replied petulantly. 'I told Marshal Keller everything, I told Major Calloway everything, I told Milton Packard of the Fort Bowie *Gazette* everything.'

Jesse eyed him shrewdly. Then, heeding his instincts, he said simply: 'Okay. Sorry to've troubled you.'

He turned and made to leave.

'What, ah . . . what exactly was it you wanted to know?' asked the clerk.

Jesse stopped. He'd guessed right, then. Much as the fellow might complain about it, he had enjoyed being the center of attention and wanted to remain so for as long as he could.

'I just wondered what happened last night,' he asked, turning back.

The clerk leaned across the counter and dropped his voice to a more confidential level. 'Not really much to tell. I was here all that evening. The only visitor Mr. Truman had was the man who killed him, that Indian-lover.'

'You sure about that?'

'Of course.'

'You were right here *all* evenin'?'

'Well, I stepped back into the office a couple of times. But I was never gone long enough for anyone to come or go without me knowing about it.'

'And the Indian-lover?' said Jesse. 'He was the only one who came in last night?'

The clerk nodded. 'I saw the body, you know,' he said confidentially. 'Before the marshal arrived, I mean.' He shuddered. 'Mr. Truman just about had his brains beat out.'

'A struggle like that would've made some noise, though, wouldn't it? Didn't you hear it?'

'No. But then, I wasn't listening for it. I was reading. I like to read. It takes me away from *this* place.'

'And you're sure no one else came in or went out last night?'

'May I ask why you think this is any of your business?'

The woman's voice took Jesse by surprise. He turned and saw Ann Truman standing halfway down the staircase, dressed head to foot in black. He looked up at her and took off his hat. 'I'm sorry, miss. I guess I was just being curious.'

He could tell from her expression that she didn't believe his curiosity was as idle as he made out. She came down the stairs slowly, the rustle of her dress accompanying her every step. She looked even paler than ever, and there were dark circles under eyes that were sore from crying. 'I know you,' she said when she reached the foot of the staircase. 'You were with the man who killed my father.'

There was no point in denying it, so

he just said: 'My condolences on your loss.'

She waved that aside. 'I asked you a question, Mr . . . ?'

'Glover, ma'am. Jesse Glover.'

'I'm still waiting for an answer.'

'I don't have one, Miss Turner. I didn't know your father at all and I hardly knew the man you say killed him. But what I *did* see of him . . . ' He shook his head and decided to be perfectly honest about it. 'I know his pa — that is, the man he thinks of as his pa — and he's a good man. I guess I just hate to think that his boy could do what everyone says he did.'

'I should have thought his own actions condemned him. My father was clutching an amulet, a small, acorn-shaped thing with Indian markings on it. They tell me the man Redwood had been seen around town wearing it.'

'You're probably right. But one thing my own father told me was that, 'til you know better, always to give the other feller the benefit of the doubt.'

'So you believe he's innocent because that's what you want to believe?'

'Until I know better, yes ma'am. As naïve as that likely sounds.'

'I saw him,' she said stiffly. 'Kneeling over my father's body. He turned and we looked each other right in the eye and then he fled. There wasn't much doubt in my mind as to who was responsible.'

'And like I say, I'm sorry for your loss. Sorry for coming in and raking it all up again. I didn't intend for you to hear.'

She stared at him for a long, uncomfortable minute. Then: 'All right,' she said. 'I'll accept your apology. But if this man Redwood didn't kill my father, who did? Who managed to enter and leave this hotel without the desk clerk seeing?'

'*Glover!* What the devil are you doing here?'

He turned as Jim Lord came across the lobby toward them, his eyes moving from Jesse to Ann and back again.

'Nothin',' said Jesse.

'It doesn't *look* like nothing,' said Lord, belligerently.

'Jim . . . ' said Ann.

Ignoring her, Lord squared up to Jesse, all his earlier affability seemingly forgotten. 'I hope you haven't been bothering Miss Turner. She's been through hell and — '

Jesse turned to Ann. '*Have* I been bothering you, ma'am?'

Without hesitation, she said: 'No. He just wanted to tell me he was sorry to hear what happened to Daddy.'

Lord immediately backed off, looking almost ashamed of his outburst. 'That . . . that's all right, then,' he said. 'I didn't mean to . . . I mean, Ann's been through a bad time. I guess I'm just a little over-protective.'

'Forget it,' said Jesse. 'Now, if you'll both excuse me, I'll be movin' along.'

He left the hotel without a backward glance.

* * *

117

Outside, he went as far as the end of the building, glanced once over his shoulder, then quickly ducked into the alley there. He followed the thorough-fare until he reached a dogtrot behind the hotel. He walked down until he reached the fire-stairs that zigzagged down the rear wall. They were coated in dust, which told him they hadn't been used in some considerable time. Neither were there any noticeable tracks in the dirt to show that anyone had used the stairs, or the dogtrot, any time recently.

But what did that really prove — if anything?

He told himself he was crazy to keep clinging to the idea that Tyler hadn't killed Truman, even though everything pointed to it. What did he know about the kid, anyway? How could any man know what another man was capable of? And yet there was gut-instinct. That, and his loyalty to Patch were enough to make him keep looking for something that might throw up another suspect.

9

The minute Zulu Sam decided to continue tracking on foot, the mustang beneath him slowed to a halt without needing to be told.

There existed a strange chemistry between Sam and the animals among which he had found kinship. Sam had no better understanding of it than anyone else. It was simply a sense of belonging, an instinct that had led him to these proud creatures in the first place. And that was strange, for in his own country his people had considered horses as the feet of the white man, and would have nothing to do with them.

Now Sam slid from the back of his mustang and subjected the land around him to a slow, penetrating stare. There was no wind, just the still, hot air and a silence broken every so often by the zip and buzz of flies. He was surrounded by chaparral-covered flats, the brush thickening around the bases of the few distant, craggy mesas and hills in evidence.

Despite his best efforts, there had been no tracks to follow. The passage of time and the elements had erased what little sign Ethan Patch had left behind him — and anyone who knew Patch knew there would be precious few clues to the direction he had taken in pursuit of his son. But Sam had never really intended to rely solely on tracks.

He lifted his chin a fraction, closed his eyes and tested the air. Behind him, the mustang shook its big head and instinctively did likewise. There was hardly any sound, and with his eyes closed his senses were focused on the scents of the air: the sage and creosote, the dust and dirt, of tough grass and plants that smelled like heated wax, and vanilla, ponderosa pine and warm rocks.

And man.

Man, and horse.

Men, and horses.

Sam opened his eyes and broke into an easy lope, headed north toward the distant mesas. The mustang reared up behind him, then went racing after him. Man and beast crossed the hard country with a dizzying sense of freedom.

He closed on the foothills, and as he drew closer he saw an almost imperceptible trail winding between all the brush. Like a dog on the scent, he followed the trail at the same mile-eating jog, the mustang falling behind him now.

The trail opened into a shallow canyon littered with light gray rocks, many balanced on top of each other to give the terrain an otherworldly feel, and spills of bright green brush. He came upon a shallow stream full of frogs and tadpoles, knelt, cupped some water and drank. The water tasted good.

The canyon was absolutely silent. A stray breeze shuffled milkweed and meriwhitica. But Sam knew that men had come this way recently. There were no tracks, save those of elk, coyote, bighorn sheep, cougars and cottontail rabbits. But there was the smell of dry wood, burned as a smokeless fire, still fresh on the air.

He stood. The mustang watched him inquisitively. Sam turned, scanned the rims of the canyon, almost blindingly white against the deep, azure blue of the cloud-free sky beyond.

He began to walk, following the winding course of the stream.

A hundred yards on a voice above and to his right growled: 'That's far enough, Sam.'

Sam halted, turned a little at the waist, raised his head.

Ethan Patch was just visible in a nest of rocks about thirty feet above him. He was carrying a Henry repeater slantwise across his chest.

'What the hell're you doin' here?' he asked. He looked whiskery, dusted, a man who right then could have chewed nails and spit tacks.

'Come to find you,' Sam replied mildly.

'You scoutin' for the army?'

'You know better than that, Ethan.'

The scout relented a little. 'I guess. Why, then?'

'We're concerned for you, Ethan. You and your boy both.'

'Who's 'we'?'

'Jesse Glover. Me. Geronimo.'

There was a stir of movement beside Patch, and a moment later a youngster Sam guessed must be Tyler Redwood showed his face. He wore the same gray suit he'd arrived in, but it was now showing signs of wear. He looked young and uncertain, and his eyes went wide when he saw the massive Zulu.

'Mind if I come up and join you?' asked Sam.

Ethan shrugged. 'Come ahead.'

Sam scaled the incline with all the grace of a cat. His horse stayed put, flicking his tail lazily to keep the flies at bay.

Ethan had chosen their hideout well. Their camp was large enough for them to keep their horses back in rock-shade, and at a high enough elevation to keep most of the canyon within sight. Sam realized that Patch had probably watched every step he'd taken since entering the defile.

Now Patch said to Tyler: 'This here's Sam. He's a friend.'

Tyler hesitated a moment, then stuck out his right hand. Sam made no move to take it, instead looked into the youngster's face and said: 'Did you kill the man they *say* you killed?'

Tyler replied unhesitatingly: 'No, I did not.'

Sam nodded. 'I believe you.' And as they shook: 'A man can lie with his tongue, but never with his eyes.'

Tyler seemed to sag a little. 'Thank you, mister . . . Sam. Now all I have to do is convince the rest of Fort Bowie.'

'Well, runnin' away wasn't the smartest move you ever made in *that* direction.'

'I panicked.'

'Why?'

'It's not every day you walk in on a dead man.'

'Is that what happened?'

The boy made a quick, impatient gesture with one hand. 'I was there, I don't deny that. I went up to speak to Truman about his plans to exploit Gaan Canyon. I was hoping to get him to change his mind.'

'How did you get past the desk clerk?'

'I told him Truman was expecting me. I knew he wouldn't see me at all if I tried to arrange a meeting beforehand.'

'So you went up to Truman's room . . . ?'

'The door was open. I knocked, looked in . . . and saw the body.'

'He was already dead?'

'I wasn't sure. But I went in, thinking that maybe I could . . . I don't know, revive him in some way.

'He opened his eyes, but I don't think he really saw me. I mean, he really didn't know who I was. He tried to say something but couldn't. He reached up and grabbed my amulet. I wear this — '

'I heard.'

'Well, he grabbed the amulet and then he had some kind of . . . I don't know, it was like a convulsion. Scared the heck out of me and I leapt back. The rawhide broke and next thing I knew he was holding my amulet in his hand . . . and he was dead.'

'What happened then?'

'There was a scream. I turned and saw a girl standing in the doorway . . . Truman's daughter. I saw at once how it must look, what with the argument I'd had with Truman the day before.' He shook his head wretchedly. 'I panicked, ran.'

'Why didn't you just go straight to Marshal Keller?'

'Folks'd been snubbin' him ever since they pegged him for an Indian-lover,' Patch cut in testily. 'He didn't think anyone would believe him.'

'He was probably right,' allowed Sam. 'So what have you been doin' ever since? You can't hole up here forever.'

'Boy'll never get a fair trial in Fort Bowie. We figured we'd ride on down to Tucson, see if things'd be any fairer for him there. That, or try to catch the real killer ourselves.'

Sam opened his mouth to speak again when he suddenly turned toward the south.

'What is it?' asked Patch.

'Sounded like gunfire,' Sam replied.

'I didn't hear anythin'.'

'A ways off,' said Sam.

'Soldiers?' asked Tyler. 'I might have known it was only a matter of time before they ran us to ground.'

'They *are* out lookin' for you,' Sam admitted. 'Officer name of Madsen leadin' 'em.'

'Madsen's new to the territory, still green,' said Patch. 'Only way he'll ever find us is by accident.'

'Anyway,' said Sam. 'It's not soldiers I'm worried about right now. It's Geronimo.'

10

Geronimo reined in and shook his head, sending a shiver through his long black hair. This was a fool's errand. No man could find the tracks of Ethan Patch if he did not want them found. Patch was one of the very few white men who knew as much — maybe more — about such matters as the Apache. That was one of the reasons Geronimo respected him.

Another was the strength of Patch's word. Once given, it was never broken. That was something he could not say for many white men.

Where Patch had earned his admiration, however, it irritated Geronimo to feel the same way about Jesse Glover. He had a powerful hate for anyone not born of Apache blood. And he did not think anyone could blame him.

When he was in his late twenties, a

Mexican colonel named Carrasco had led four hundred soldiers down into the camp where he had been living, just outside Janos, Chihuahua. They had waited until all the men had gone into town to trade, and then they'd snuck in, killed the guards, stole the Apaches' horses and weapons, burned their supplies and all but wiped out the women, children and old people left behind. Even now, sixteen years on, Geronimo's throat tightened at the memory. His wife, Alope, his three children, his mother . . . they had all been killed.

His lifelong hatred of Mexicans had started then. After that he and his companions attacked and slaughtered them wherever they found them.

Eventually Mangas Coloradas had sent him to the tribe of Cochise, hoping to temper his lust for revenge, and he had learned from the older warrior to wait, bide his time, to fight only when the odds favored him.

But still that restless, reckless fire burned within him. And as the years had progressed, so he had learned to hate the whites, too, for they were all of the same stock — they gave words meant to be broken, made promises that were empty but sounded good.

It irritated him that Jesse Glover was like Patch — a man upon whom he could rely. He didn't *want* to rely on Glover. He wanted to push all the whites and the Mexicans out of Apache country. But that was hard to do, and becoming harder all the time. Geronimo did not wish to live in an uneasy peace, always waiting for the next treacherous act of the whites. Sooner or later the Apache would have to make a stand. It would be better to make it now, than later. But Cochise and others like him didn't see it that way. And so they branded him, Goyahkla, a fool, a hot-head, one who might well end up causing more harm than good.

His fists clenched. Where was Patch hiding, anyway? The question was almost impossible to answer, for Geronimo suspected that Patch had never truly hidden from anyone or anything in his entire life. So how was he supposed to —

A rifle shot cracked through the midday heat, rolling like thunder. Geronimo's pinto pranced around even as Geronimo himself twisted to see where the shot had come from. On the far side of the plain, distorted by the quivering air, he saw a group of riders. Soldiers? Who else would be so keen to shoot at him?

He jabbed his heels into the pony's flanks and the animal took off running. The ground flowed beneath man and rider, for there was no option in such a situation but to retreat until they could meet again, with the odds, next time, in Geronimo's favor.

He did not really expect the riders to pursue him. There was too great a distance between them and there was too little to be gained by chasing one lone Apache. And yet the riders immediately kicked their own horses to speed and began to swarm across the plain in his wake.

Now Geronimo was certain they

were soldiers. No one else would be so foolish as to pursue so small a target on so hot a day. Neither was he especially concerned, for the day he could not outrun the yellow-legs had yet to dawn.

With a rush of exhilaration, he gave a wild cry that was pure joy. Let them come! He'd wear them out and send them home sweated and lathered and —

A flurry of shots snapped across the badlands as his pony swept up across an incline stubbled with mesquite. Instinctively Geronimo dropped his head lower between his shoulders, but knew they would never hit him, or anything else for that matter, from the back of a galloping horse.

The pony dug in and continued to scale the slope. Geronimo glanced back, surprised to see how drastically his pursuers had cut the distance between them. For the first time he knew a moment of disquiet, for no soldiers ever rode that well.

Then he saw that they were not soldiers.

They were Indians.

Geronimo hauled rein. His pony reared, turned, planted itself midway up the incline, waiting for orders like the well-trained animal it was. Geronimo raised his chin, looked at the riders below, scowled. They wore the white-stripe war paint of the Apaches. Their horses were decorated with colorful circles and palm-prints. But they were not Apaches.

They were Navajo.

Similar in many ways to the Apache, they were nonetheless long and bitter enemies of the *N'de*, the People. But what were they doing here now? They should be on their reservation to the north and east, in the land white men called the Four Corners.

Geronimo wondered briefly if there was a new war brewing, one between the Apache and the Navajo; whether or not the Navajo were trying to move in and do what the whites had so far failed to do and push them out.

Then the riders — he estimated there were *kah-tin-yay*, thirty, of them — drew rein, stood bunched at the foot of the hill, peering up at him . . . and another threw a rifle to his shoulder and fired a shot.

Dust spurted up around his pony's hoofs and he yanked the reins hard, turned and jabbed the animal into motion. The pony climbed higher, as behind and below him, Geronimo heard the Navajos begin to yip and scream with the thrill of the chase. More shots ripped through the air. The pony climbed higher, the jagged rim, stark yellow against the cloudless sky, coming closer with every leap.

Then Geronimo felt something punch into the pony's lathered haunch, felt a shiver pass through the animal itself, and even as it staggered he knew that, more by chance than anything else, one of those wild shots had hit the animal.

The pony went down with a painful grunt. As it dropped flat with legs kicking, Geronimo threw himself sideways. He hit the slope running, sprinted for the cover of some rocks about thirty yards away with bullets chasing his every step.

He glanced behind him. The Navajos had spread out, were now charging up the slope as fast as their mounts could carry them. He cursed himself for not recognizing them sooner, for assuming they were bluecoats and underestimating them because of it.

But there was no time for recrimination. Bullets whipped through the air. How nothing hit him he would never know. The rocks rapidly drew closer. If he could make cover, he had a chance. He could pin them down, wound or kill some, make the rest think twice before coming after him. And then, when the chance came, he would slip over the blind side of the hill and vanish as only an Apache could —

He was almost to the rocks when a fusillade tore through the air. Stone chips exploded from the rocks ahead and flew back at him. Geronimo knew a moment of white-hot pain in his face and faltered. Moments later blood streamed down his face, into his eyes, and he knew that one of the splinters had hit his forehead, disorientating him.

He heard the Navajos screaming louder. They knew they'd hurt him and were anxious to hurt him some more.

Temporarily blinded, he continued heading for the rocks, misjudged the distance and caught himself on an outcrop, opening a gash in his left thigh.

Then the ground beneath him trembled with the pounding of hooves, and he rose shakily, his senses spinning. He knew they had him, knew they were even now surrounding him. He smelled their sweat and that of their horses, heard the horses stamp and shift and fidget, heard a couple of his captors chuckle in anticipation of the torture to come.

He tried to fight his imbalance, tore his old Manhattan revolver from his belt. There was a crack as someone used a lance to knock the weapon from his grasp. As it skittered down-slope Geronimo felt the impact of the blow right the way up to his shoulder.

At last he ran a forearm up across his eyes, clearing the blood from them.

The Navajos looked down at him, showing him no more mercy than he would have shown them. He glared back at them, defiant, knowing nothing of fear but filled to brimming with a raging, impotent fury.

One of the Navajo stabbed a Walker Colt down at him. From this angle the gun looked huge. A brown thumb eared back the hammer. Geronimo tensed, knowing he had nothing to lose by trying to rush the warrior. To go down fighting was better than the alternative.

Then a voice behind Geronimo said, '*Ndaga!*'

The Navajo's forefinger eased off the trigger.

Geronimo turned to face the speaker. He was sitting his horse to the west, and the sun was behind him, flickering across one thin shoulder, casting the rider himself in silhouette.

'You're the one they call Goyahkla,'

the rider said in English.

He giggled, high and hysterically.

Geronimo lifted his arm to shield his eyes against the sun and get a better look at the man.

He was surprised to see that the fellow was white, though his skin had been tanned to the color of chocolate. He was tall and emaciated, with a low brow, widespread eyes, a thin nose with flared nostrils and a broad mouth. He wore a collarless deerskin shirt, loose-fitting breeches of some thin, powder-blue material and moccasins. At his waist was a gunbelt, in the pocket of which sat a sleek Model Army Colt.

But it was the man's eyes that were most arresting. His left eye was deep, bloodshot brown. His right eye was missing, in its place a milky off-white orb. And as he took off his sombrero and sleeved his withered face, Geronimo saw a scalp that was a maze of tortured-and-healed flesh from hairline to crown, fringed by bone-white hair that was brittle and fuzzy.

It was the head of a man who had been scalped and lived to tell of it.

'And you,' Geronimo replied at last, 'are the one they call Tchin'dih.'

The grin that spilled across the white man's face was smug and satisfied.

'Yeah,' he said. 'We met one time, up around Turkey Creek.' He giggled some more, as if at some personal joke. 'Looks like this is our lucky day, boys.'

He jabbed heels into his horse's sides. The animal plunged forward, knocked Geronimo to his knees. Before he could recover, the man called Tchin'dih tore his Colt from its pouch and struck down with the barrel. Geronimo went stiff and then flopped to the dust.

Tchin'dih turned to his companions, and reverting to Navajo, announced: 'Next place we hit, we'll leave his body fresh-killed behind us. An' if that don't convince the army that the Apaches're cuttin' up rough, nothin' will!'

11

At first there was no sound, no vision, nothing. And then, gradually, Geronimo realized he was coming back from a dark place, that he was belly-down across a walking horse, that his feet were free but that his hands had been tied at the wrists with pigging strings — tied expertly.

His head throbbed to the pace of the horse's every step. He felt sick, and was ashamed at his weakness; ashamed also that he had allowed himself to be taken captive by these Navajos he had mistaken for soldiers and foolishly attempted to outride. He remembered being caught, being hit by the man who looked more like death than death itself, the one called Tchin'dih.

He wondered what Tchin'dih was doing here now. Again it came to him that perhaps the Navajo were declaring war on the Apache, that they were determined to take Apache lands for their own, and at once the usual, fiery anger that was never far from the surface began to course through him.

He lifted his head a little, saw through the stygian web of his hanging hair that he was the last in the strung-out line of riders. The horse upon which they had thrown him was being led by a Navajo in a patterned shirt, who was carrying the lead rope loosely wound around one hand. Ahead of him the rest of the Navajos were riding loosely in their buckskin saddles, Tchin'dih leading them across this flat, barren plain.

He closed his eyes, tried to work on the knots that bound his hands at the wrists. It was, as he had known it would be, a futile exercise. But it was not in his nature to go quietly. If he was to be a prisoner of the Navajos, he would fight them every step of the way.

He tried to gauge where they were going. He had no idea. But they rode warily, even though the chance of running into anyone else was slim in this vast wilderness.

After a while Tchin'dih called two names. Two Navajos heeled their mounts up alongside him. He said something to them and gestured with one clawed hand. The Navajos nodded and forged out ahead.

They pushed on. Geronimo tried to think of a way to escape, but tied as he was there was little he could do.

An hour passed. The heat hammered at him and his thirst increased. He knew better than to ask for water. That would only guarantee that they made him go without. Still concussed, he drifted off to sleep without realizing it until the pounding of hooves brought him back to consciousness. He looked up just as the scouts came galloping back in from the south.

Tchin'dih drew rein. The others followed suit behind him. The scouts made some sort of report, gesturing back the way they had just come. A ripple of excitement seemed to trickle down the line and Tchin'dih himself giggled that high-pitched, insane laugh of his. Geronimo scowled, wondering what was afoot. Tchin'dih turned in the saddle and called back to his companions. Geronimo caught the words *T'àà* and *bilagàana*. A white man — presumably, someplace up ahead.

Tchin'dih issued more orders. His Navajo was almost fluent. He spoke it so quickly that Geronimo missed most of it, although he heard enough to get the gist. They were going to attack and kill the white man.

More orders were snapped, this time aimed at the brave who was leading Geronimo. He was to hold back and follow at a distance. Then Tchin'dih and the others kicked their horses to speed and soon vanished into their own dust and the fading light of a day Geronimo had expected — until now — to be his last.

★　★　★

The sun was just dropping behind the distant hills and Jesse was still two miles from home. He'd spent longer in town than intended, but wasn't really any closer to discovering the truth about Cord Truman. Still, the day hadn't been a complete waste of time.

He'd been walking back down to Gravey's Livery, where he'd left his horse, when he ran into Jim Lord again. Instinctively he'd tensed, expecting another confrontation. But to his surprise, Lord had said: 'You ready to have that drink now?'

' . . . I guess.'

He and Lord crossed Main and went into the first saloon they came to. Business was slow and they more or less had the place to themselves. When Jesse asked Lord to name his disturbance, however, Lord shook his head. 'First one's on me.'

'It's me who's beholden to you, remember?'

'Forget it,' said Lord. 'Everyone wants to buy you a drink when you're a survivor. It's about time I bought one for myself.'

He ordered whiskey and they took their glasses over to a corner table.

'I behaved like an ass earlier,' said Lord. 'When I saw you and Ann together in the hotel lobby, I mean.'

'I reckon you've got every right to be protective of her right now.'

'It's more than that,' Lord said.

'Want to talk about it?'

Lord studied him for a long beat, considering it. Finally he said quietly: 'It's eating me up, Glover . . . the fact that I was the only man to survive Devil's Canyon.'

'Just thank your lucky stars you *did* survive it.'

'You don't get it,' Lord said. 'You want to know why I didn't die with the rest of them? Because I hid, that's why. I ran and I *hid*, because I didn't want to die and I certainly didn't want to die at the hands of a savage. I saw what they did to the men with me and I turned yellow.'

Jesse sipped his whiskey, weighing his

reply before offering it. 'You did what you had to do to survive,' he said at length.

'I wish that was true. As it stands, I think death would have been preferable to the guilt I'm living with right now.'

Something suddenly made sense to Jesse — or leastways he thought it did. 'So you're tryin' to prove that you're not a coward,' he said. '*That's* why you bought into that fight I was havin' with that Haskell hombre.'

'And I guess it's why I braced you the way I did when I thought you were bothering Ann Truman,' Lord confessed sheepishly.

'You've got nothin' to prove, Lord.'

'To myself I have.'

'Well, there's nothin' I can do to stop you feeling that way. But for what it's worth, you made your decision. Now you've got to live with it. No use goin' around pickin' fights to show how tough you are. Best you just try to make whatever's left of your life *count*.'

'And that's it?'

'Sorry if you were expectin' somethin' deeper,' Jesse said. 'No one knows what they'll do in a situation like that 'til it happens. But you did what you did, and you can't go back and undo it. So live with it, and make sure you make your life count for somethin'.'

'To make amends,' Lord murmured thoughtfully.

'If that's the way you want to look at it.'

Lord sat back. 'Maybe you've got something there. Maybe there *is* something I can do to make my life count.' He smiled for the first time. 'Thanks, Glover. For not judging me and for giving me the best advice I could have had.'

'Which was . . . ?'

'To quit feeling sorry for myself,' the surveyor replied.

* * *

Now Jesse sat a little straighter in the saddle to ease the knots in his back.

He'd helped Jim Lord solve his problem, but was no closer to helping Ethan Patch solve *his* — if indeed there was anything *to* solve. Maybe Truman's murder really had happened the way everyone seemed to think it did.

An arrow suddenly zipped past his face.

Startled, he turned just as the Indians came pouring through the trees to his left — ten, twenty, maybe more of them, barely visible in the approaching dusk, the din they made screaming turning the peaceful evening silence into a memory.

Jesse jabbed the sorrel and it leapt forward into a flat-out run.

Behind him, the Indians curved out onto the trail in a strung-out line. Jesse risked another look over his shoulder. One of the leading riders was holding a bow crosswise above his horse's bobbing head, an arrow nocked in the buffalo sinew string. He hooked his Colt from leather and threw a shot back at his pursuers in an attempt to make them give up the chase.

It didn't work.

Beneath him the ground rose and then fell away rapidly. As he and the horse plunged down the slope his stomach seemed to drop right out of him. He faced front again, scrunching low as arrows flew around him, as if that might actually keep one from hitting him.

The trail twisted sharply to the left, between high rocks. The horse followed it with fast-drumming hooves. Jesse threw another shot along his back trail, trying to figure exactly where he was, and how far he still had to go before he could reach the relative safety of his ranch. But even as he thought it, he wondered just how safe he would be. Outnumbered by around thirty-to-one, in a half-built cabin with a tarpaulin for a roof . . . flaming arrows would make short work of that, and then what? He'd be forced to make a break for it, die in a hail of lead . . .

At least I'll make 'em know they've

been in a fight, he told himself grimly.

That made him think of Lord. Were these sonsofbitches the same bunch who'd killed those men in Devil's Canyon? The Apaches were keeping to themselves right now, as Patch had said, so who else could it be?

The ranch came into sight then, about half a mile distant. Jesse's heart sung briefly, for under cover he had a better chance than he did out on the plain. But the ranch looked so small, so isolated. Any respite would be brief, at best.

The horse surged into the yard. Jesse yanked on the reins and the creature came to a dust-spraying halt. He threw himself out of the saddle, all too aware of the howling Indians right behind him, how close they were, how fast they were closing the distance, and tugged on the reins.

The horse, scared by all the noise, by the arrows that kept *thwipping* around them, tried to fight him, almost dragged him off his feet. But there was no time for that. He swore at the horse, hauled again and this time the horse allowed him to lead it toward the cabin.

The Indians boiled into the yard, dust billowing as they spread out. The noise was tremendous. Jesse swore, still yards from the cabin door, and knew he was never going to make even that dubious protection before they shot him full of arrows.

Making up his mind, he let the horse go free, and as it turned and fled he tore the Winchester from its scabbard and jacked in a shell.

'*Come an' get it!*' he bawled, and slammed the stock to his shoulder and fired at the first rider to come into his sights.

The long gun boomed and a whole fusillade accompanied it, or at least that's the way it seemed. His bullet went wide, he knew it did, but two other saddles emptied in as many seconds, and he thought with a kind of disbelief, *Those shots came from the cabin, from someone inside the cabin!*

The shots took the Indians as much

by surprise. The charge stopped in its tracks, and all at once the Indians were fighting to get their milling horses back under control and grab cover.

More shots rang from the small, glassless windows. A horse neighed, went up and spilled its rider. A lance embedded itself in the dirt directly in front of Jesse and he told himself he needed to get under cover pronto. He turned, ran for the cabin just as another flurry of muzzle flashes exploded from the windows. The man who'd come off the horse suddenly spun, corkscrewed himself into the earth and lay still.

Jesse burst into the darkened cabin, managed breathlessly: 'Who — ?'

A deep voice said softly: 'Trust you to bring trouble home with you.'

'*Sam?*'

'And us,' said Ethan Patch. 'Me an' Tyler.'

'Now find yourself a place to start shootin',' advised Sam. 'They' comin' again — an' this time they mean business.'

12

Geronimo gathered himself in readiness, awaiting his chance to act. The man holding the lead rope turned and looked at him. Immediately he feigned unconsciousness. The Navajo, short but sturdy in his patterned shirt and breeches, stared at him for a few moments, then sniffed and turned back toward the direction his companions had taken.

Ten minutes passed, slow as molasses. Then, in the distance, came a flurry of gunfire. The man holding the lead rein stiffened and raised his chin a little as he looked in the direction of the shots, as if it would somehow help him to see what was happening out there beyond the brush-topped hills.

Geronimo knew he would get no better chance — that if the ambush went as planned Tchin'dih and the others would be back soon. He shifted weight, slid down off the horse onto his feet.

The Navajo heard him, slight though the noise was. He turned, his eyes widening.

Geronimo powered forward, threw himself at the Navajo even as the brave tried to drag a knife from his belt.

They both went flying off the far side of his horse in a tangle. They hit the ground hard, Geronimo on top of his opponent. He clubbed the man in the face, hard and without mercy. The Navajo's nose broke and blood gushed. He struggled beneath Geronimo, but Geronimo hit him again and again, each tied, two-handed blow fueled by a building, blinding rage and each one more powerful than the last.

Finally the Navajo's eyelids fluttered and the eyes themselves rolled up into his head. It was of no consequence to Geronimo whether he was dead or merely unconscious. He drew the knife from the man's sash, turned it awkwardly in his hands and quickly sawed through his bonds.

Then he pushed up off the brave and quickly checked him for other weapons. He relieved the man of a Cooper Pocket double-action revolver in .31 caliber. Then, tucking gun and knife into his own waistband, he jogged across to where the horses waited nervously close by.

Before the nearest animal could balk and shy away he sprang up onto its back and gathered the reins. In the distance another flurry of shots sounded more like firecrackers. For a moment he was undecided. For an Apache there was no shame in running, if it meant being able to come back and fight when the odds were more favorable. But it came to Geronimo that he should tail these interlopers and their white-eyed leader, find out more about them. Besides . . .

He suddenly realized where he was. The ranch of *Scan-To* lay not far from here. And much as he disliked the one called Glover, they were brothers in blood. If *Scan-To* was the white man the Navajos had seen and decided to kill . . .

His mind made up, he heeled the horse after the Indians.

*   *   *

The Navajos drew back, regrouped, licked such wounds as they had, then split up and came in again, this time from every direction. Arrows *thunked* solidly into the walls of the cabin, a couple finding their way in through the windows. In the darkness shadows skittered from one spot to another. Jesse drew a bead on one, led it a little way, then pulled the trigger. The Indian ran straight into the bullet, went over onto his back and lay still.

Then, all at once, it fell silent again and the Indians melted back into the night.

Silence stretched long and taut. Tyler whispered: 'Is that *it?* Is it *over?*'

'Not yet,' said Patch. He had moved to the rear door, was kneeling to one side of the small window there, rifle in his big hands.

'Who are they?' asked Sam.

'The same sonsofbitches who hit those men in Devil's Canyon'd be my guess,' said Jesse.

'Did you get much of a look at them?'

'Funnily enough, I was too busy runnin' for my life at the time.'

'Boy,' muttered Sam, 'you sure are sour this evenin'.'

'It's been that kind of a day. Beaten up this mornin', shot at tonight.' Jesse took his eyes off the yard for the briefest moment. 'What are you fellers doin' here, anyway?'

Tyler said: 'We've been trying to figure out a way to prove my innocence. In the end there was only one way to do it — to turn me over to the authorities in Tucson, and hope for a fair trial. We stopped by here first to let you know, but you weren't around, so we decided to wait.'

'Lucky for me you did.' Jesse looked around. 'Where's Geronimo?'

'That,' said Sam, 'we don't know. We

figured he'd meet us back — '

Before he could finish Tyler yelled: '*Here they come again!*'

★　★　★

In the scrubby darkness behind the cabin, a lone Navajo grinned coldly. Tchin'dih's plan was working perfectly. With Tchin'dih and the others keeping the hated *bilagàana* busy at the front of the cabin, he had been able to sneak in close and quickly build the small fire that was his part of the mission.

The Navajo's name was Naalnish and when the small fire took hold, he quickly scooped up the bow he had set aside and slid an arrow from his deer-skin quiver. Just behind the notched head of the arrow he had tied a small, resin-soaked *tow*, or bundle, of dry grass and kindling.

He nocked the arrow, then dipped its head into the small flame. At once the resin caught light. Wasting no time, Naalnish straightened, drew back the string and fired the arrow. It flashed toward the cabin and struck the wall. There was a spill of glowing embers . . . and then the fire began to catch.

Grinning still wider, Naalnish took out another arrow, nocked it —

There was a sound behind him.

A sound that should not have been there.

Even as he began to turn, another man reared up behind him. The newcomer's muscular left arm came up around his neck, yanked back his head. Almost in the same moment the knife he held in his right hand swept across Naalnish's throat. There was an instant of blinding pain, an explosion of light behind Naalnish's screwed-shut eyelids . . . and then the Navajo dropped bow and arrow and went limp.

Geronimo dropped the body as if it were nothing, wiped the knife on his breeches and then slipped it back into his waistband. Grave-faced now, he snatched up the bow, almost tore the quiver from the dead man and then jogged toward the side wall, where he ripped the flaming arrow from its niche and tossed it away.

As he ran off through the brush he was watchful at all times. The Navajos were still peppering the front of the cabin with bullets and arrows. The sound masked any noise he made ghosting from one patch of cover to the next, always working his way around the spread so that he could come upon them from the rear.

After a while he stopped dead in his tracks. He smelled horse on the faint breeze, and scanned the darkness. A whinny carried to him above the sound of gunfire, and he smiled coolly.

He made his way between some rocks until he came to a shallow, rock-littered arroyo where the Navajos had left their horses. One man had strung a rough picket line and was dividing his attention between the animals and the battle going on to his northwest.

Geronimo nocked an arrow, drew back the string and released it. The

160

shaft smashed the Navajo in the back and shoved him face-first into the dust. Even as the Indian kicked out his final moments, Geronimo padded silently down into the arroyo and swiftly cut through every slipknot with which the horses had been tied to the rope.

Waving his hands wildly, he then yelled: '*Yaah! Deyaah! Deyaah!*'

The ponies needed no second urging. Lurching away from him, they collided in their haste to quit the gorge, then poured out onto the flats like a flash flood.

Behind him, Geronimo caught a sudden lessening of gunfire. Good — the Navajos had heard him, heard the sound of their departing horses. In moments now they would break off the attack on the cabin and try to round them up.

Geronimo would be waiting for them.

Nocking another arrow, he sprang up out of the arroyo and into the cover of some rocks. When he found the vantage he was after, he sank to his haunches and waited.

His patience was rewarded less than thirty seconds later. The first of the Navajos came sprinting along the trail, clumsy in his haste to discover what had become of their horses and the man guarding them. Geronimo surged upright, drew the bowstring taut and fired. The arrow slammed into the oncoming Indian's upper breastbone, just below the trachea. The man gave a gasping wheeze, then pirouetted to the ground.

Three more Navajos came hard on the heels of the first. Lips tight, expression murderous, Geronimo nocked another arrow, fired, one more, fired, a third, fired.

The first arrow missed its target. The second hit one of the Indians in the leg and he stumbled and screamed. The third also missed.

Geronimo silently cursed the poor workmanship of the Navajos. Genuine Apache arrows *never* missed their targets.

He nocked another arrow even as one of the Indians on the trail fired at him.

Aiming just below and to the left of the muzzle flash, Geronimo loosed the shaft and was rewarded by a gurgling scream.

But now the rest of the Navajos were retreating from the ranch yard — too many even for Geronimo to think about taking on at once. He fired another arrow into the coming pack — someone howled — then he turned, leapt over a spill of rocks and vanished into the darkness, with arrows, lances and bullets chasing him away.

13

'*Don't shoot! It is me!*'

Geronimo strode into the yard a few minutes later, broad shoulders back, square chin up, nostrils flared, the very picture of pride and power. He got about halfway across the yard when a voice called from the cabin: 'That you, Goyahkla?'

'Who else?'

'Better get in here pronto.' Geronimo recognized Patch's voice and raised an eyebrow. 'I got a notion them other fellers'll be back afore long.'

'They will not return,' the Apache assured them. The door now opened and he went inside, casually tossing the bow and the remaining arrows onto the table. 'They will spend the rest of tonight rounding up their horses — or trying to.'

Jesse scanned the yard one final time.

'You spooked 'em?'

'And killed many,' Geronimo replied. He flashed the fingers of his right hand four times.

'Twenty?' Jesse asked skeptically. 'My, you *were* busy.'

'You were not doing so well by yourself,' the Apache said. Then: 'They are Navajo.'

Patch came forward. 'What the hell're the Navajo doin' in this neck of the woods?'

'This I do not know. But they are led by a man called Tchin'dih.'

Sam turned away from the window. 'How do you know all this?'

Geronimo opened his mouth, hesitated, then said: 'I spotted them earlier, when I was looking for Patch. I followed them. This I saw with my own eyes.'

'They didn't get the drop on you then,' said Jesse.

Geronimo eyed him sharply. 'Why would you say such a thing?'

'That's quite a bump you got on your noggin,' Jesse replied. 'But it's had a while to heal. And if I didn't know better, I'd say you been tied at the wrists recently, too.'

Ignoring him, Geronimo studied Tyler. 'You are the one who killed the man in town.'

'I'm the one they *say* killed the man in town.'

'You are also the one who spoke for the Apache.'

Tyler nodded.

'Then your heart is good.'

Patch said: 'Could be these are the varmints who killed them fellers out at Devil's Canyon.'

'Likely,' agreed Sam. 'But why do they want to make it look like it was the work of the Apaches?'

'They are our enemies,' said Geronimo.

'Hell, half the country are your enemies,' said Jesse. 'That's the thing with you Apaches. You don't try real hard to make friends.'

'They want to blacken us before the yellow-legs,' Geronimo continued. 'They want to get the yellow-legs to destroy us once and for all, so that they can take our lands.'

Jesse raised an eyebrow at Patch. Patch shrugged. 'Could be. One idea's as good as another right now. Let's go back to this here Tchin'dih.'

'You know him, Ethan?'

'The Navajo called him Tchin'dih because it's their word for *ghost*, and that's pretty much what he looks like. Real name's Hoyt Willard. Was a *Comanchero* afore he took up with a Navajo squaw name of Haloke. Then he settled down, bought himself a little spread southeast of here.'

'And now he's ridin' with 'em?'

'It makes sense he's ridin' with the *Navajo*,' said Patch. 'He's got a powerful hate agin the Apaches.'

'He is an evil man,' said Geronimo. 'A year ago, he refused to allow some of my brothers to shelter during a bad storm. All they asked was to shelter in his barn until the storm passed. He said no, and threatened them with a rifle if they didn't leave. There were heated words, and then he shot one of my brothers dead.'

'These here 'heated words',' said Patch, 'they wouldn't have had anythin' to do with Willard's Navajo wife an' baby, now, would they?'

'This I do not know,' Geronimo said vaguely.

'Well, my understandin' is that the Apaches insulted Willard's wife, an' Willard lost his temper. He shot your man, that's true. But there was no call for what followed.'

'Which was ... ?' asked Jesse, although he thought he could guess.

'They attacked Willard, blinded him in one eye, scalped him, left him for dead. Then they raped his wife and killed the child, a little boy. They wrecked his place, stole some of his cows and ran them back to the reservation.'

'Only Willard wasn't dead.'

'He was as near death as made no difference. Would've died for sure if it hadn't been for his woman. She patched him up, best she could. But the Apaches'd hurt her bad, she was all broke up inside, and she died shortly after.

'Well, you know the Navajo. They plant their dead real quick, with no real ceremony. But they do have one custom — after they're all through mournin' their dead for four whole days, they abandon the house where the death happened. That's what Willard did. He buried his folks and then took off, a crazy man, went to live with the Navajos in Canon de Chelly. That's when they started callin' him Tchin'dih.'

'But what's he doin' here, now?'

'If I didn't know better,' said Patch, 'I'd say he's gettin' revenge.'

'Then we better make sure Calloway knows what's happenin',' said Sam.

'If he'll listen to reason.'

'We'll soon find out,' said Jesse. 'We'll ride on in to Fort Bowie at sun-up tomorrow. We'll tell Calloway all about this Willard character — and then bodyguard Tyler all the way to Tucson, and make sure he gets a fair trial.'

* ★ ★ ★

They spent a restless night, half expecting the ghost and his renegade Navajos to come back and press the attack some more. But by the time false dawn started streaking the sky Jesse decided Willard or Tchin'dih or whatever the heck he called himself, had decided to leave them alone. He was probably still out there somewhere, searching for the horses Geronimo had scattered.

A few hours earlier, after Sam said he'd take the first watch and the others had settled down to try and sleep, Jesse had looked Geronimo in the eye and said: 'Thanks. You pulled our beans out of the fire tonight, Goyahkla.'

The harsh lines of Geronimo's face had slackened a little at that: he hadn't expected thanks for his actions, but you could tell he appreciated it — even though he tried hard not to show it.

'White men,' he had replied with a shake of his head.

Now Jesse stepped out into the new day. Three dead Navajos painted with Apache markings littered the yard. He grimaced, knowing he'd better get them planted before the heat got to them and they started attracting buzzards and coyotes. The arroyo where the Navajos had picketed their horses was the best spot — far enough from the cabin, and with enough rocks to cover the graves and keep the predators away.

He stood over the nearest corpse and looked down at the body. Beneath the distinctive white-stripe war paint the Indian's features were unmistakably Navajo. Stifling his distaste, he grabbed the corpse by the wrists and started to drag it out of the yard. The dead man's heels left shallow grooves in the sand.

'Need some help, there?'

He glanced up. Standing in the cabin's bullet- and arrow-riddled doorway, Tyler looked so different to the boy who'd arrived on the eight o'clock stage that never rolled in before nine. He'd folded his shirtsleeves back up over his muscular forearms, removed the celluloid collar from his shirt and had unbuttoned his vest. His fair hair was mussed, his face burned to copper by the time he'd already spent outdoors. He looked a little older too, a little less smooth around the edges.

'Sure.'

It wasn't a job to relish, but to his credit Tyler strode over, took the dead man by his ankles and together they carried him out of the yard toward the trees and the arroyo beyond.

'Why does it have to be this way, Mr. Glover?' he asked after they'd set the body down beside the others Geronimo had killed — which, Jesse noted, came to nowhere near the twenty Geronimo had claimed the night before.

'What way? And it's Jesse.'

'This,' said the boy, gesturing to the dead men. 'Killing, or being killed.'

'That,' sighed Jesse, 'is somethin' I wish I knew. But I don't. It's just the way it is out here.'

'But that doesn't make it right.'

'Of course it doesn't. If there was a way to change it, I'd sign up like a shot.'

'There is,' said Tyler. 'It's called talkin'.'

'The Apaches're all through with talkin'. So are just about every other tribe on the plains. Us white men're good at makin' promises, Ty. We ain't so good at keepin' 'em. But that's not to say we're the only ones at fault. We're not.'

'I understand that. But what's needed is someone who can go between red man and white, whose word is good for all. A man like that could broker peace.'

As they entered the yard again and picked up the second body, Jesse said: 'I've tried it. Bein' that go-between you're talkin' about. It didn't work, leastways not for long.'

'But it might,' said Tyler. 'If another man tried it.'

Jesse eyed him speculatively. '*You?*'

'Why not?'

'Two reasons I can think of,' said Jesse. 'One, right now you're about as green as unripe pumpkins. You got to get some bark on you before your word'll carry any weight with anyone, save the folks who know you best. And two — you don't owe the Apaches a thing.'

'That's where you're wrong.'

'Oh?'

'I hated it, at first. Living among the Apaches, I mean. I was just a kid, scared, alone. All I thought about was getting away, but somehow the chance never came. Besides, where would I have gone, anyway? So I tried to bide my time and somewhere along the way I got used to it, the Apache way of life. At first, when Pa — Ethan — rescued me, I was glad. Then he sent me out west, and what I saw there made me . . . '

'Go on.'

'It made me wish I was back with the Apaches.' Tyler drew breath. 'Theirs is a simpler way of life. Everyone knows his place. Oh, they treated me rough, sure. But there wasn't any beating. See my ears, how they're pierced? The squaw who adopted me did that, so I'd only hear the right things and do as I was told. That was the closest I ever came to being punished, and the only reason she did what she did was for my own good. That amulet Truman tore off me . . . my adopted mother gave it to me to ward off evil. Doesn't look like it worked much, but that was the intention, that's how much she cared.

'The men were about the same. I might've been chastised, but I was never hit. That's not the Apache way.'

'I know.'

'Yes, I suppose you do. Well, the short of it is — I hated it until I didn't have it any more. And then I missed it like you can't believe. My own father, my natural father I mean, was always too busy with the way station to pay me much mind. It wasn't like that with the Apaches. The man who adopted me, his brothers, his father, they all took turns teaching me right from wrong, how to hunt, tend livestock, make weapons . . . practical stuff a man can use throughout his life. In that fancy school pa sent me to, I was shut away in a classroom and forced to learn Latin and Greek, philosophy and literature! Oh, he meant well, and the last thing I want is to sound ungrateful, but . . .'

'But you'd have sooner stayed where you were.'

Tyler nodded.

'That's why you came back?'

'Partly. I wanted to thank Pa. Whatever he did for me, he did with the best intentions. But also, I wanted to see if I could somehow go back.'

'That's the one thing no one can do, Ty,' said Jesse, thinking of Morning Star.

'But just suppose *I* could? Suppose I could go rejoin the Apaches for a while, finish learning what they started teaching me all those years ago. If I could gain their trust, I could turn that fancy education of mine to their advantage, speak for them in Washington.'

Jesse looked at him for a long moment. 'You've got it all worked out, haven't you?'

'I haven't thought about much else since I was sent to California.'

'There's just one little problem right now — Truman.'

'I didn't kill him, you know.'

'I never said you did.'

'But you wonder. You're bound to.'

'Tyler, if Ethan believes you, *I* believe you. An' you know somethin'? It might be worth savin' you from a hang-rope to see just how well you do with the Apaches.'

For the first time in too long, Tyler actually smiled. 'Well,' he said, 'the sooner we get these bodies buried, the sooner we can — ' He saw that Jesse was no longer listening to him, but instead staring out across the flats. 'Jesse?'

'We got company,' Jesse said softly.

14

Tyler turned in the direction Jesse indicated, narrowing his eyes until he could just make out a small group of riders through the quivering air, coming in off the flats. 'The Navajos?' he asked.

'Not unless they've taken a fancy to Army blue.'

By the time Lieutenant Madsen led what was left of his patrol into the yard, Geronimo, Sam and Ethan had all come outside.

One look at the patrol told its own story. Ten men had ridden out — Madsen, Sergeant Farley and eight enlisted men. Only Madsen, Farley and three troopers walked their mounts back in, and they looked badly beaten.

Madsen himself looked white as chalk. He seemed barely able to sit straight in his saddle. There was an angry bruise on the left side of his face, and blood was seeping slowly through the bandage around his right bicep. He stiffened when he saw Geronimo and automatically reached for the Colt at his hip.

Jesse hurriedly stepped forward. 'Forget that,' he snapped. 'You're on my land now an' you're among friends — and that goes for all of you. Just step down off that horse before you fall off it, lieutenant.' And then, even though he figured he already knew the answer, he added: 'What the hell happened to you, anyway?'

Madsen turned around. 'Dis . . . mount,' he managed. 'See to the . . . care of your horses . . . then yourselves.'

Farley snapped: 'You heard the Lieutenant!'

'We were . . . attacked,' said Madsen, dismounting carefully as, behind him, his men did likewise. 'About . . . three o'clock this morning. Damned Apaches came after our horses. Killed two sentries before one of my men raised the alarm. Then they were all over us. Lost five men all told.'

He looked away before Jesse could see the way emotion made his face twitch.

It was ridiculous to tell Madsen not to be too hard on himself. It had been his patrol, and the safety of his men had been his responsibility. It made no difference that he was as green and untried as most of his men.

So all Jesse said was: 'Get your men quartered in my barn, Lieutenant. They look worn out. But you ... I've got somethin' here I want you to see.'

*   *   *

To give him credit, Lieutenant Miles Madsen held his silence until Jesse finished speaking. Then he looked down at the bodies laid out in the arroyo, still awaiting burial, and said: 'So you're telling me these Indians ... they're *not* Apaches.'

'Nope. But that's what they want you to *think* they are.'

'They *look* like Apaches.'

180

'Could you tell an Apache from a Navajo, Lieutenant?' asked Patch.

'I — ' began Madsen. Then, expelling a defeated breath: 'I guess not. Not with any certainty.'

'Well, these're Navajo, all right, painted for war just like Apaches. We figure they're the band that killed those fellers out in Devil's Canyon.'

Madsen glanced meaningfully at Geronimo. 'And I'm supposed to take your word for that?'

'It's true. This feller we told you about, this here Willard, he's got a powerful hate for the Apaches. We figure he's out to stir up trouble until you soldier-boys declare war on 'em once and for all.'

'Well, he's going the right way about it,' the lieutenant sighed. 'All right. We'll ride in to Fort Bowie together and you can tell Major Calloway what you've just told me.'

Jesse snorted. 'I thought that, too — at first. But Calloway wouldn't believe me if I told him the sky was blue.'

'Could you blame him?'

'What's that supposed to mean?'

'Look at the company you keep, Mr. Glover. One of the most notorious Apaches of them all. A man wanted for murder. And as for you . . . ' He shook his head at Sam. 'I'm not even *sure* what you are.'

'You're not tryin' awful hard to win friends here, Lieutenant,' muttered Jesse. And then, as an idea struck him: 'But there's one sure way we could convince Calloway, and that's to bring Willard in ourselves.'

'*What?*'

'We can do it,' said Sam, warming to the notion. 'Between them, Patch an' Goyakhla can pick up an' follow just about any trail. If we back track Willard from where he hit you an' your men just before dawn, we can hit 'em when they least expect it.'

Madsen was quiet for a moment. Patch said: 'You lost five men, Lieutenant. You can replace four of them with us.'

'Don't forget me,' said Tyler. 'You

lost five. Take me as well and you've *gained* five.'

Jesse glanced at him. 'You don't have to be part of this, Ty.'

'Yes I do,' the boy replied grimly. 'If I'm to try and help the Apaches, I'll have to prove myself to them sooner or later — if your people at Fort Bowie don't hang me first. Fighting their enemies is as good a way as any to do that.'

Jesse nodded, said: 'You'll do to ride the river with, I reckon.'

'You will fight?' Geronimo asked Madsen.

'Alongside you misfits?' countered Madsen. Then he seemed to relax somehow, and even found it within him to smile coolly. 'Heck, yes. If my men feel about this as I do — and I'll be very surprised if they don't — yes, indeed.'

* * *

Hoyt Willard clenched his teeth and rocked back and forth, moaning. His head wouldn't quit aching. It ached a lot these days, so much and so often that sometimes it became as much a part of him as blinking or breathing. But every so often the ache turned into something more, a nagging, pulsing, throbbing pressure across the top of his ruined scalp and down around his temples, and the sight in his one good eye would blur, the eye itself water, and then there was nothing to do except pour rotgut whiskey down his throat to deaden it.

The trouble was, he was all out of rotgut whiskey right now.

He continued to hug his skinny frame and rock back and forth, the moan escaping from between his thin lips a low, agonized keening. He could hardly see more than fuzzy shapes now, and the rushing in his ears sounded more like a downpour.

'Haloke!' he called suddenly. 'Haloke!' And he thought, *Where is that damn' woman, anyway?*

A tiny voice inside him said: *She's dead.*

Dead?

They killed her, Hoyt. The Apaches.

Willard exhaled and sagged a little. 'Course they did. How could he have forgotten that? They took his precious little Haloke and they violated her and then they killed her, just like they killed his baby son.

Around him, his little army of Navajos watched him warily. They had known him first through his dealings with them as a trader and later through his marriage to Haloke. When he had returned to the Navajo they had been happy to care for him. But his sickness had changed over the months, and it was rumored that he had been touched by Etsay-Hashkeh, the Coyote, who sometimes made crazy dogs that bit men and made them crazy as well. They didn't call him *Shi Cho' Adehn* — crazy — to his face, of course. But they called him Tchin'dih, because he looked like a ghost.

Some of the *Diné*, the Navajo people, had decided after a time to avoid him.

He was bad medicine. Others had continued to nurse him back to some semblance of health because they were too scared of what might happen if they didn't. And some of the young men, who were sick of the way they had been treated by the whites, found something in Tchin'dih's ramblings that appealed to them. The violence in him, the hatred, the willingness to kill . . . it was these characteristics that struck a chord within them. They did not see him as mad. They saw him as having been touched by the gods.

In his more lucid moments, Willard understood this, and exploited it. It reminded him of the old days, the days before Haloke, when he and his fellow *Comancheros* had ruled this vast land and traded with the Indians and made their fortunes and their reputations. These young men who hung on his every word and cared for him when the headaches grew too strong, they were his troops, and he was their commander.

'Where's Haloke?' he called now.

No one answered. All continued to watch him closely, knowing that before long the pain would make him shriek and scream and writhe until it passed again, and Tchin'dih was once again well enough to lead them against the hated whites and the hated Apaches.

The tiny voice inside him said again: *She's dead.*

Dead?

They killed her, Hoyt. The Apaches.

Willard nodded. *That's right. They did.* How could he have forgotten something like that?

At last he realized that the headache was fading, that his vision was clearing, that he was thinking somewhat clearer, and to the surprise of all he suddenly let loose a long, bubbling giggle.

He remembered that there had been dissent following their attack on that ranch the previous night. So far they'd had it all their own way. They'd killed and not *been* killed. Then, last night it had all gone wrong. Six dead . . . seven, including the brave he had left in charge of their prisoner, Goyahkla. It had sobered the others, the young ones who had believed they were invincible until bullets and arrows had shown them otherwise. And then, when they'd been forced to retreat and spend half the night tracking down their horses . . . that had added insult to injury, humiliation to fear.

Some of them had started muttering about calling it a day, going back to Canyon de Chelly. The cowards! Willard had stopped that kind of talk in its tracks. He'd turned on them with such speed that a couple had actually flinched.

'No one quits!' he'd hissed. 'We see this *through!*'

But somewhere along the line they'd elected one of them to be their spokesman. Willard hadn't liked that, either. The brave they'd chosen was called Yiska. He was tall for a Navajo, his raven-black hair framing a flat, grave face the color of coffee.

'We need to mourn our dead,' he said.

Willard stalked back to him, the others hurriedly clearing a path for him. He stopped in front of Yiska and said: 'We don't have time for that. We got to round up our horses, an' then we got to go back an' make them sonsabitches pay!'

'Or lose yet more of our number,' muttered Yiska.

Around them, some of the others mumbled agreement.

That's when the headache started. It was as if the rage that suddenly coursed through Willard lit a flame in his brain. He lashed out, backhanded Yiska. The brave stumbled backwards, fell to one knee. His lip was split, and blood glistened wetly in the chilly moonlight.

Someone whispered: '*Ałt' aa la' hóníí' 'o'oołts 'id!*'

Yiska heard it, heard the truth of it. He *had* been insulted. He could take it, and live with the shame, or he could make the man who had insulted him take it back.

He sprang to his feet, ripped a knife

from its sheath at his hip, snarled: '*Ch'iidii!*'

It was exactly what Willard wanted and he drew his own knife. After everything that had happened tonight, it would feel good to kill something. Might even help this damn' headache.

But then one of the watching Navajos pointed off toward the northeast and said: 'Look!'

It was if time suddenly froze in mid-tick. Willard and Yiska continued to glare at each other. Then, slowly, Willard straightened to his full height and said, without taking his eyes off his opponent: 'Where?'

'There,' said the man who had raised the alarm. 'A fire.'

Their differences temporarily forgotten, Willard, Yiska and the others turned in the direction indicated and saw a tiny prick of amber light in the distance. Two such lights . . .

Campfires.

'Who is it?' whispered a brave called Sani.

Willard shoved his knife away. 'We'll find out.'

It turned out to be cavalry, a small patrol of just eight men, a sergeant and a lieutenant. Their officer must be an idiot. Their campfires were too big, too bright, and there was one more than they really needed. There were only two sentries. Out here there should have been at least four.

And they had horses.

Willard's headache was still faint enough to allow him to think reasonably clearly. He saw the benefits of attacking the soldiers. A quick, easy victory would bolster the flagging spirits of his little band and quell the mutiny that was threatening to erupt. They would acquire the horses they needed. And if they were careful the attack would be blamed on the hated Apaches.

His giggle had been soft, then.

The sentries had been dispatched silently, their bodies dragged into rocks and dumped. But some of the horses had balked at the unfamiliar smell of the Navajo, and that had betrayed them. Someone had yelled the alarm, and the night suddenly exploded with gunfire.

Most of the troops were green, and despite the yelled orders of their sergeant, nothing could make them defend their camp worth a damn. Better yet, Willard's men threw themselves into the battle with a recklessness he found heartening. They had already been beaten once tonight. Pride would not allow it to happen a second time, even if it meant fighting to the death.

The patrol suffered heavy losses until the young lieutenant in command managed to pull the survivors back to high ground. But by then the damage had been done — the patrol had virtually been wiped out, and most of the horses were Willard's for the taking.

The victory over the long-knives had satisfied the Navajos. Now they were anxious to kill again, and Willard was pleased. But first . . . first he had to let this damn' headache pass. Then he could plan their next move.

'Haloke!' he cried, again forgetting that his wife was dead. 'Where are you, woman?'

And he giggled some more.

15

As soon as he spotted Jesse and the others in the far distance, Ethan Patch brought his own mount to a halt on the saguaro-studded prairie and waited for them to reach him. When they finally drew rein, Lieutenant Madsen said: 'You've found them?'

'They're restin' up in a draw about two miles east,' said Patch. 'There's eighteen of 'em, plus Willard, an' it looks like they've rounded up just about all the hosses Geronimo scattered last night. Won't get a better chance to take 'em than right now.'

Madsen squinted at the country up ahead, where rust-colored mountains stretched from one horizon to the next. 'Have they posted guards?' he asked.

'One, at the mouth of the draw,' said Patch. 'But I can soon take care of him.'

'Very good. When you're done, we'll

enter the canyon and I will call upon the man Willard to surrender.'

'He won't, you know,' said Jesse.

'After what he did to my patrol,' said Madsen, 'I hope he *doesn't*. Still, we want to make sure we take *some* of them alive. They've got a lot to answer for.'

'Fair enough,' said Patch, 'though my instinct'd be to give *them* as much chance as they've given everyone they've hit so far.'

He turned his mount back the way he'd just come and the others fell in behind him.

Though badly shaken by their first, disastrous taste of action, Madsen's raw recruits had seemed willing enough to go back and settle accounts for their lost comrades. By the time Jesse, Sam and Tyler had finished piling rocks over the dead Indians, they'd seen to their horses and weapons and were looking as nervous as hell but grimly determined to go get the job done.

They rode in silence for a couple of

miles until Sam used his *assegai* to point the way ahead. 'Rider comin' in,' he called. 'Fast.'

Patch twisted around. 'It's Geronimo.'

At once the tension within them climbed a notch. If Geronimo had left his position in the draw, something was up.

The Apache reined up so fast that his horse slithered a little on lowered haunches. Without waiting he snapped: 'They are getting ready to move out.'

'*Damn!*'

'Did they see you?' asked Jesse.

Geronimo's glance was withering. They both knew that if Geronimo didn't want to be seen, there was no way he would be.

Madsen gathered his reins. 'Which way were they headed?'

'North and east.'

Patch considered quickly. 'That'd take 'em up toward Kyle Doniphan's place — the KD Connected.' He eyed Jesse. 'Reckon Willard's figurin' to hit the ranch today?'

Jesse nodded. 'Gotta be. It's the only place out that way.'

'Can we cut them off?' asked Madsen.

'We can try,' said Patch. 'It'll mean pushin' these horses hard, but if we can do it, maybe we can hit 'em as they leave the canyon.'

'I think there's a better way,' said Jesse. 'What's the best way to reach the KD Connected from that draw, Ethan?'

'By way of Firestone Canyon. Only alternative is goin' up over the mountains.'

'Then we'll swing out ahead an' wait for them at Firestone Canyon,' said Jesse. 'Get 'em bottled up there, catch 'em in a crossfire — then force the sonsofbitches to surrender.'

Madsen considered briefly. There was no time for anything longer. At last he nodded briskly, and gathering his reins he called back: 'All right, you men. You heard Mr. Glover. Now let's *move out!*'

★　★　★

Hoyt Willard felt good — the best he had in days. But it had been that way with him ever since Haloke had . . . he frowned, momentarily confused. She *was* dead, *wasn't* she? Sometimes he had a hard time accepting that, like it was some kind of mistake. But that's how it was — the darkness would grow in him and so would the rage, and then would come the headaches and the only way to cure the headaches was to kill.

And now he was on his way to kill some more.

The pain had eventually put him to sleep, and the sleep, brief though it was, had chased away the pounding in his skull. Next time he awoke he knew what was needed. He needed to cause more pain and suffering, because only by causing pain and suffering in others could he ease the pain and suffering in himself.

There was a ranch to the northeast of Firestone Canyon, small, run by a family named Doniphan. It was a nice, soft target that would give them an easy victory. And if Willard remembered rightly, Doniphan had a couple of handsome women out on that spread of his, his wife and her sister.

The women held no interest for Willard himself. The only woman for him had been Haloke. But the young bucks with him . . . the women would be part of their reward for sticking with him.

The morning warmed up. Willard rode wary. He and his ragtag army had come here to stir up a hornet's nest. Could be there were patrols out looking for him even now. Or rather, looking for the *Apaches*. He had been most particular about that. Every attack he had staged so far was meant to throw blame on them.

Of course, there had been no help for the bodies they'd left behind. That was the only possible way he could have fouled up. But he knew white men as well as he knew red. Few could tell the difference between a Navajo and an Apache. Fewer still would ever think to look for such a difference.

All in all, he was pleased with the way things had gone, and with what he had been paid to achieve. When this was over, he could just sit back and watch the army do its best to wipe out the entire Apache nation. Now *that*, he thought, was vengeance.

'Tchin'dih!'

He squared his shoulders, suddenly aware that he had been too immersed in his thoughts. Now he looked around, saw Sani pointing at something beyond the next rocky rise.

It was a single strand of smoke.

Willard drew rein, checked his surroundings. Yep, this was it — the Doniphan place, KD Connected — right the other side of Firestone Canyon.

He turned his horse so that he could address his companions. He told them that the whites were up ahead, that they wouldn't suspect a thing. They were easy meat, and they would die this day under Navajo hands.

He saw the eagerness in their faces, in their eyes. They were like rabid wolves, and that's just what they were — the wolf-pack he had made of them. 'Up ahead is what the Messicans call *Piedra Lumbre* Canyon — Firestone Canyon to me. That's where we'll find the Doniphan spread . . . an' Doniphan's women!'

His cackle was high and shrill, the babbling laugh of a man hopelessly beyond true sanity.

'Let's ride,' he said.

He led them toward a great, mis-shapen gouge in the red, scrubby hills directly ahead.

Firestone Canyon was about a quarter-mile wide and maybe three miles long. Its craggy red walls slanted away to east and west from a reasonably straight, *caliche*-littered trail, each sloping rise covered in saltbush and hackberry, brittlebush and kidneywood.

As he led them into the canyon, Willard felt his heart begin to beat in time with the sudden *pock-a, pock-a* of their horses' hooves. Anticipation of the violence to come made the blood sing in his ears. He'd suffered as bad as a man could, and saw no reason why he shouldn't make others suffer just as much — especially if that suffering brought about the hunting, killing and eventual extermination of the hated Apaches.

He closed his fingers around his reins, reached down and eased the Colt in its holster. He glanced over one scrawny shoulder. Strung out behind him, his warriors were checking their own weapons.

His lips parted in a cold grin.

Then —

He didn't know what it was. Just a feeling . . . a bad one.

He scanned the western slope, scanned that to the east, saw nothing untoward and yet . . .

Somethin's wrong.

He didn't waste any more time questioning it. He just turned his horse and bawled: '*Ji-din-nes-chanh!* Retreat!'

Midway up the western slope Lieutenant Madsen screamed: 'Fire at will!'

At once chaos filled the canyon.

Three Navajos were knocked out of their saddles in that first withering fusillade. Horses began to dance and rear. Instinctively Willard drew his Colt and thumbed off three retaliatory rounds.

Yiska screamed his defiance at their enemies and sent his mount galloping toward the western slope, guiding the animal by knee-pressure so as to leave his hands free to work his Winchester.

It was a crazy move that would only end one way, and it did just that. The horse went down first, shot in the chest, and Yiska flew madly over its head. He slammed against the ground and rolled sideways an instant before the animal could land on top of him.

The brave leapt up, heedless of everything save the need to buy time for his companions to leave the area. He snatched up the fallen Winchester, worked the lever —

A bluecoat wearing the single gold shoulder-bar of a lieutenant suddenly broke cover, stood tall and stabbed a

Cavalry Colt at him. Yiska screamed defiance as the officer snap-aimed and fired. Then the Navajo flew backward with a .44/.40 shell clogging his windpipe.

Now men were breaking cover all along the slope, raining lead down on the confusion below, and the startled Navajos were fighting back. Willard saw that their ambushers were just a small mixture of soldiers and civilians — even Goyahkla himself!

With rage boiling in him, Willard underwent a change of heart. '*Al-tah-je-jay!*' he screamed, and sent his horse charging at their enemies. '*Woltah-al-ki-gi-jeh!*'

Sani had already reached the foot of the slope. Willard saw him strike one of the soldiers square on the head with an axe, saw the soldier drop limp and lifeless at the feet of his prancing horse. But Sani's moment of triumph was short-lived. A tall man in greasy buckskins — dimly Willard recognized him as Ethan Patch — came out of nowhere and threw a long-bladed knife overarm. It spun through the air, embedded itself in Sani's chest and the young Navajo somersaulted backward off his mount, hit the ground and lay kicking.

Willard threw a shot at one of the civilians, a youngish man with fair hair. He knew a moment of satisfaction when his target spun and fell, clutching his left shoulder. He snap-aimed, intending to finish the boy off, but just before he could fire another of his braves surged past, spoiling his aim.

The brave — Willard recognized a vicious-tempered boy named T'iis — sent his mount charging up the slope, a lance held high, his arm held back, ready to throw.

Jesse came out from behind some brush with his Winchester held by the barrel. As the Navajo went by he swung the rifle and smashed the rider out of his saddle. The Navajo flew back through the air, the lance slipping from his grasp. He hit hard, grunted, rolled once, grabbed a gun from his waistband.

Jesse turned the Winchester, worked the lever, fired twice. The Navajo grunted, hunched up under the impacting shells and seemed to twist himself into the ground.

Not far from Jesse, Geronimo shot another Navajo and looked around. Riderless horses were milling everywhere. Dust floated in billowing clouds. The air was tainted with the stink of blood and cordite, and copper-skinned bodies wearing Apache war paint lay scattered everywhere.

A bullet sang past Willard's head, sending his sombrero spinning and exposing his ruined scalp to the blinding sunlight. Willard stiffened, saw the youngster he'd just wounded thumbing back the hammer on his handgun and trying for another shot at him.

He bawled: '*Ji-din-nes-chanh!* Retreat!'

Slamming his heels into his horse's flanks, he twisted the animal away to the east and gave it its head. As he went, Zulu Sam caught a glimpse of his startlingly white hair and muttered: '*Willard!*'

He broke cover and went sprinting down onto the flats in pursuit.

Another Navajo spilled sideways off his shot horse. Willard had to slow and swerve in order to avoid a collision. As he rode on, the Navajo snatched up his fallen tomahawk and threw it at his nearest target — Sam. Sam dodged the weapon, slammed one big shoulder into the Navajo, sent him spilling again and ran on.

The Navajo cursed, cast around, saw a fallen rifle and grabbed it up, intending to shoot Sam in the back. He was just slapping the stock to his cheek when someone behind him bellowed: '*Gusano!*'

The Navajo turned just as Geronimo, who had followed Sam down off the slope, snatched up the fallen tomahawk and threw it hard.

It struck the Navajo in the center of the forehead and he collapsed, the rifle dropping from his quivering fingers.

Willard, meanwhile, was heading back the way he'd come, knowing it had all gone wrong, that he hadn't been quite as clever as he thought he'd been. He felt the pressure building inside his skull again, and swore. *Not now!*

And where the hell was Haloke?

He glanced over his shoulder, saw Sam surging after him, running back-straight, arms pumping, muscular legs taking almost impossible strides. He told himself the black man could never catch up with him, it wasn't possible . . . but the way he just kept coming, dark face grimly determined —

Willard dragged on the reins. His horse stumbled, turned at his urging. Facing Sam side-on, the man they called a ghost took aim and emptied his Colt. Sam threw himself sideways, rolled behind a rock, came up on the far side with something spinning at the end of his raised right hand.

Willard had never seen anything like it. It was a length of rope weighted at all three ends with smooth, fist-sized rocks.

He wasn't to know it was a *bolas*, that weapon favored south of the border, where experts could use it to bring down game by allowing the weights to wrap the rope around its feet.

He fired again, realized the gun was empty and yanked the horse back around — and that was when Sam flung the *bolas*, sending it through the air toward the fleeing renegade.

It caught Willard in the back of the neck and the weights wrapped it tightly around his throat, until at last the weights themselves could turn no further and slapped Willard in the face. The man was knocked sideways and fell from the saddle to land, winded, beside his skittish mount.

Even as he opened his single good eye and started to rip the contraption from his throat, Sam's shadow draped across him. Willard froze, looked up at the Zulu and figured he'd never seen the like before.

'Quit your strugglin', Willard,' Sam said grimly. 'It's over.'

16

It was coming on sunset when the battered column entered Fort Bowie's main drag and walked their horses slowly down toward the garrison. Lieutenant Madsen rode at its head. Jesse came next, alongside Geronimo and Zulu Sam. Finally came all that was left of Madsen's original patrol, just two men, plus Ethan Patch and Tyler Redwood, whose shoulder-wound had been patched, albeit crudely, before they'd said their farewells to the Doniphans at the JD Connected. Between them, these four rode point, swing and drag on the wounded and beaten survivors of Hoyt Willard's renegade army — including Willard himself.

Marshal Keller came out of his office, wondering just like everyone else who stopped to watch them pass, what the hell had transpired. Among the onlookers was Jim Lord, his arm curled around Ann Truman's trim waist. When someone identified Tyler with a pointed finger and a: *'That's him! That's the Injun-lover who killed Truman!'* Lord and the girl exchanged a look, and Lord said softly: 'I think we'd better get down there and see what's going on.'

Word rippled out ahead of them, and by the time they rode across the Fort Bowie parade ground and Madsen called a halt outside the admin block, Major Calloway and his adjutant, Lieutenant Travers, were waiting for them.

Madsen threw up the smartest salute he could manage, given his arm wound. Calloway looked at him, at the men behind him, and said: 'What's this all about, Lieutenant? Where's the rest of your patrol? And that . . . that man there . . . that's *Geronimo!*'

'And a better man I've yet to fight alongside,' returned Madsen. 'As to the rest of my patrol . . . ' He paused briefly, then: ' . . . they're dead, sir. But what you see here is the remains of the band that killed them. Them and the surveyors out at Gaan Canyon.'

'What?'

Arriving just in time to hear that, Lord and Ann exchanged a glance.

'It's a long story, Calloway,' said Jesse, nudging his horse up alongside Madsen's. 'An' we're hot and tired and thirsty and hungry. Dismiss these men, have the prisoners placed in your stockade an' then you'll get your answers.'

Calloway eyed him disdainfully. 'The day I take orders from a civilian — '

'*Do* it,' said Patch, suddenly speaking up. 'An' while you're at it, we want you to convene a hearin' into the murder of Cord Truman. First thing in the mornin' ought to do it.'

'That's a civil matter,' Calloway replied.

'Yeah,' said Jesse. 'But in the absence of a duly-appointed circuit rider, you got the right to convene a hearin'. We're askin' you to do it tomorrow, so we can draw a line under this damn' business once and for all.'

'Are you that anxious to see this

young man hung?' Calloway demanded smugly.

'Just convene the damn' hearin'.'

Calloway considered it for a moment, then said: 'Lieutenant Travers — have the prisoners taken away . . . including young Mr. Redwood there. Lieutenant Madsen, dismiss your men and join me in my office immediately. The rest of you . . . ' He eyed Jesse and his blood brothers dubiously. ' . . . I suppose you had better come in as well, if this story's as long as you say it is.'

And Ann Truman squeezed Jim Lord's arm and whispered worriedly: 'We need to talk.'

★   ★   ★

For once, Calloway was as good as his word. Overnight the saloon was cleaned up and a table was set at the far end of the room from which the major would preside over the hearing. Twelve ladder-back chairs were set in two rows of six along the left-hand wall for the jurors.

More chairs were set out facing the table for the benefit of those townsfolk who wanted to attend . . . which was pretty much the entire population of Fort Bowie.

Jesse, Sam and Geronimo arrived early, Geronimo clearly ill at ease among so many Apache-hating whites. Patch joined them shortly afterward, his seamed face carved in worried lines. As the saloon filled up, Calloway himself arrived and went directly to the desk, upon which he set a fat, dog-eared bible. He threw one baleful look at Jesse and sat down.

A hush descended when Jim Lord and Ann Truman arrived. The girl was still dressed in black. Lord still wore a black armband around the sleeve of his gray suit. They took the last two seats in the front row, which Jesse had made sure to reserve for them.

Lieutenant Travers and two guards followed them in, with Tyler, hand-cuffed, between them. The boy looked pale, and not just from the further ministrations of the army surgeon the previous evening. He was told to take the seat to the left of Calloway's desk and did so.

Finally Lieutenant Madsen arrived with Hoyt Willard.

The renegade's presence caused a particular stir. No one could figure what he was doing there. He was told to take the chair that had been set up to Calloway's right. With a shrug and a secretive little giggle he flopped down and stared up at the wagon-wheel chandelier overhead, seemingly oblivious to everyone around him.

The jury was selected and sworn in, after which Calloway drew his Colt, upended it and tapped the butt on the desk for order. Silence claimed the saloon. The major said: 'We are here to establish the guilt, or otherwise, of the man seated to my right, whose name is Tyler Redwood. If the jury finds him guilty, it will be my unfortunate duty to pass sentence . . . and we all know what that means, in a case of murder.'

Jim Lord glanced down at the girl beside him.

'For that reason,' Calloway continued, 'I feel obliged to remind the jury that if there is any doubt in their minds as to this man's guilt, they have to find him innocent.'

'He did it, all right,' muttered someone at the back of the room.

Calloway spotted the speaker immediately. 'It's Tom Haskell, isn't it? You have a reputation for trouble, Mr. Haskell, but we won't stand for it here. Marshal Keller — have that man removed!'

Haskell's eyes went wide. 'You can't do that!'

But it seemed that Calloway could, and did.

After Haskell was thrown out, Calloway said: 'Mr. Redwood. Please rise and face the court. You are charged with the willful murder of Mr. Cord Truman on the eighteenth instant. How do you plead?'

'Not guilty.'

'Not guilty to the willful murder of

Cord Truman?' asked the major. 'Are you saying you committed the crime in *hot* blood . . . that it happened by accident?'

'I'm saying I didn't do it at all,' Tyler replied resolutely.

'If it was an accident,' persisted Calloway, 'the court might be persuaded to show leniency.'

'I didn't do it,' said Tyler. 'And I'll be damned if I'll say I did, and didn't mean to, just to avoid a rope.'

'But we have *evidence*, Mr. Redwood. We have a witness who saw you crouching over the body. We have an amulet the dead man tore from your neck, presumably during the struggle. We have the fact that you fled town, which is most certainly *not* the act of an *innocent* man. Mr. Redwood, we have just about everything we need to hang you.'

'*He didn't do it!*'

Impulsively, Jim Lord jumped up, his fists clenched tight, his expression wretched. 'I did it,' he said, 'and I'll not let another man take my punishment!'

The saloon burst to life and Calloway had to tap the butt of his gun again to restore order. 'Hush, now! Hush, I said! I think you'd better explain yourself, Mr. Lord — and do so under oath!'

Ignoring him, Lord said: 'We were arguing that night about a . . . a personal matter. The argument got out of hand and . . . I didn't mean to push him, but I did and . . . '

His voice trailed off.

Into the silence Jesse stood up and said: 'Still trying to do the right thing, Jim?'

'What's that?'

Instead of replying directly, Jesse looked at Ann. 'Why don't *you* tell us, Miss Truman?'

For a moment he didn't think she was going to reply. But then she rose slowly to her feet, almost as if in a trance, and clutching her purse before her, croaked: 'I did it.'

'Ann — '

'No, Jim.' And then, louder, firmer:

'For some time now I have been at odds with my father over . . . over Jim, here. I love Jim. He is a good man, and I want no other. My father wanted more for me, certainly more than a divorced man who is . . . somewhat older than me.

'After what happened out at this place, Devil's Canyon, I realized just how close I had come to losing Jim, and so that evening I went to see my father so that we might forget our differences and settle the matter amicably, once and for all. But when I entered his room, I found that he was busy in the adjoining bathroom. I decided to wait for him to come out, and whilst waiting noticed a number of papers spread across his bed. Without really meaning to, I read part of the top sheet. It detailed a plan to . . . somehow clear the way for my father's company to acquire mining rights in Gaan Canyon.'

'Go on,' said Jesse.

'For God's sake, Glover — '

Once again Ann talked Lord down, speaking almost to herself, and with

219

relief to share the secret she had held for too long. 'He had hired agents to undertake a search for someone who . . . who would commit a number of atrocities in this region and make it appear as if the Apaches were to blame. His thinking was that the government would then take steps to wipe them out and leave him free to establish a presence in Devil's Canyon without the Indian trouble that would otherwise go with it.'

'And his, ah, hired agents . . . ?' prompted Calloway.

'They found that man over there,' she said. 'M-Mr. Willard. Apparently he had considerable hatred for the Apaches and was happy to take my father's money to . . . to carry out the work.'

'So you killed him,' said Calloway.

'No,' she said. 'I . . . I *did*. But it was as you just said. It was done in hot blood. You see, he had deliberately arranged that first attack in Devil's Canyon as a means of . . . '

She started crying.

Lord said: 'What she's trying to say is that Truman tried to kill two birds with one stone. That attack out at Devil's Canyon would set his plan in motion . . . and at the same time it would get me out of his daughter's life — permanently.'

'Miss Truman?' asked Jesse.

'When he c-came out of the bathroom I . . . I confronted him with the evidence. I had always known he could be a hard man in business, but never did I dream that he could be quite so ruthless.

'We argued, and I . . . I slapped him. He lost his temper — he has . . . had . . . always been a man of quick temper — and took me by the arms and tried to push me from his room. I struggled and pushed back and . . . and he fell, and caught his head.

'I thought he was dead. I mean . . . he wasn't breathing, as near as I could see, and neither could I detect any heartbeat. I don't know, I just . . . it was all so unreal that I couldn't think properly. I was in a kind of daze.

'I went back to my room. I was shaking, dizzy, felt sick. It was my . . . hope that my father's death would be seen as an unfortunate accident — for that's really what it was — but before I raised the alarm I decided to go back into his room and remove and destroy all those damning papers. It's ridiculous, isn't it? I k-killed him, and yet I had no desire to besmirch his memory.

'B-but by the time I did return to his rooms the . . . Mr. Redwood here, he was kneeling over my father, who was not dead, as I had believed, but died even as I entered the room. I screamed, and Mr. Redwood ran . . . and now I knew no one would believe that he had died by accident.'

'So you let Tyler take the blame,' murmured Patch.

Unable to confess as much, Ann could only nod. Then she looked up at Jesse and said: 'How long have you known the truth?'

'I didn't,' he replied. 'Until now. But I did know that no one other than Tyler entered or left the hotel the night your father died. Lord here was staying at the Harper House. He told me that himself, when we agreed to have a drink together. To me, that meant whoever killed your father was already staying at the hotel. That way they had no need to pass the clerk that evening. They were already there.'

Lord took the girl in his arms and gently forced her to sit down again. She buried her face in his chest and wept softly.

Jesse said: 'Just to make it all legal-like, I had Willard here brought in to testify to bein' hired by Truman; that it was him an' his boys did all that killin' and raidin', and weren't no doin' of the Apaches. That right, Willard?'

Willard finally took his eyes off the wagon-wheel chandelier and rose slowly to his feet. He looked more like a ghost now than ever. He glanced around, his good eye fixed on the bible on the table before Calloway, and he stepped across to pick it up.

'I swear that's just how it was,' he said.

And then, before anyone could do anything about it, he threw the bible aside, scooped up Calloway's Colt and stepped behind the startled major.

'An' now,' he called, 'I'm gonna do what I should'a done months ago!'

And cackling at his horrified audience, he said: 'I'm gonna be reunited with my Haloke again!'

He shoved the barrel of the Colt into his mouth and pulled the trigger.

THE END

Epilogue

Partway up into the Dragoons, with the stronghold of Cochise still miles ahead, they spelled their horses for a while on some lush flatland and Jesse walked off a ways to study the splendor of the country he had chosen to settle in. While Sam saw to the horses, and Geronimo paced restlessly, eager now to return to his people, Ethan Patch and his adopted son shared a few final words together.

'You sure about this, Ty?'

Tyler absently reached up and touched the acorn-shaped amulet that had been returned to him. 'My mind's set on it, Pa. Been set on it ever since you first sent me west. The Apache way of life . . . it's a hard one, but a good one — by my lights, anyway. It's a life I want to live, and they're a people I want to help.'

'It won't be that easy, you know.'

'No. But nothing that's worth having ever is.'

Patch cracked a rare smile, and something moved in his pale blue eyes. 'Jesse got it right, didn't he?' he said. 'You really *will* do to ride the river with.'

It had been an eventful few days. Ann Truman had been formally arrested for the murder of her father and Major Calloway had sent a wire to the territorial capital, requesting a retrial, this time presided over by a judge who would be better able to understand all the legal ramifications of the girl's crime. It was widely suspected that she would get a reduced sentence because of her age, sex and emotional state at the time of Cord Truman's death . . . not forgetting the fact that she was already being punished by having to live out the remainder of her days knowing that she had killed her own father.

Jim Lord had vowed to wait for her, no matter how long her sentence. Jesse believed he would do just that.

More importantly, Calloway had finally seen sense and wired the War Department with the recommendation that the Truman Copper Consortium be forbidden from establishing a mining community on land that was sacred to the Apaches. The trouble such an act was likely to cause would far outweigh the plain good sense of simply respecting the Apaches and their right to Gaan Canyon.

Which just left the matter of young Tyler.

He had claimed that living among the People again would serve him well when he finally went East, to Washington, where he was determined to fight for the Apache cause in the very heart of the country's government. They'd all looked to Geronimo when he said that, and Geronimo had studied the boy for a long time before finally nodding solemnly.

'You have shown yourself to be a powerful warrior,' he had said. 'Now you have the chance to show yourself to be a powerful *ally*.'

So it was settled.

They reached the stronghold sometime around late afternoon. It was a haven of peace and harmony in an otherwise hard and unforgiving landscape. As they rode in, Jesse was torn between wanting to see Morning Star one more time and knowing that seeing her again would only bring more pain than pleasure.

Word had gone ahead of them, as it always did, and the people gathered to welcome Geronimo and the others. Jesse, Sam and Patch fell back as Geronimo accompanied Tyler to Cochise's lodge, and sat their mounts in silence as Cochise studied the youngster for long moments before finally nodding, as if satisfied, and saying: '*Dagoteh*. From this day forward you will be called *Nitis* — friend.'

Tyler's shoulders dropped in relief. '*Iheedn*,' he said formally. 'Thank you. I will try always to live up to the name.'

As the formalities were conducted and Tyler was absorbed into the tribe,

Jesse allowed his gaze to wander. Cochise's people had gathered in the clearing to see and evaluate this new member of their community, and a sea of copper faces studied him with curiosity and interest.

And there, among them, he suddenly saw Morning Star.

His breath caught. His heart raced. And as he looked at her, and saw the way she was looking at Tyler, he remembered what she had said to him when he'd suggested that Geronimo would be a better prospect for her.

'No,' she'd replied. 'But one day, someone will be.'

He wondered if it that someone would be Tyler.

As if reading his mind, Zulu Sam said softly: 'Can't win 'em all, Jess.'

After a time, Geronimo and Tyler came back across to join them. One look at Geronimo's expression showed that he, too, had noticed how Morning Star had looked at Tyler. He swung lithely astride his pony and said:

'Come, brothers. Our job here is done.'

Tyler reached up and clasped hands with Sam, then followed suit with Jesse. 'Thank you for everything,' he said, clearly emotional at being taken in by the Apaches.

'Forget it,' replied Jesse. And then: '*Sadnleel da'ya'dee nzho.*'

Long life, old age, everything good.

He turned his mount and he, Sam and Geronimo rode away without a backward glance.

'Is he all right?' asked Tyler, watching them go.

'Who, Jesse? Sure.'

'He just seemed a little . . . I don't know. *Sad*, almost.'

'He'll get over whatever's ailin' him,' Patch predicted. 'An' the next time trouble comes to these parts, him, Sam, Geronimo . . . '

He nodded, almost to himself.

' . . . those three'll ride again.'

We do hope that you have enjoyed reading this large print book.

Did you know that all of our titles are available for purchase?

We publish a wide range of high quality large print books including:
Romances, Mysteries, Classics
General Fiction
Non Fiction and Westerns

Special interest titles available in large print are:
The Little Oxford Dictionary
Music Book, Song Book
Hymn Book, Service Book

Also available from us courtesy of Oxford University Press:
Young Readers' Dictionary
(large print edition)
Young Readers' Thesaurus
(large print edition)

For further information or a free brochure, please contact us at:
Ulverscroft Large Print Books Ltd.,
The Green, Bradgate Road, Anstey,
Leicester, LE7 7FU, England.
Tel: (00 44) **0116 236 4325**
Fax: (00 44) **0116 234 0205**

Other titles in the
Linford Western Library:

CLANCY'S LAST WAR

Terrell L. Bowers

Some crimes are too heinous to go unpunished. Morgan Clancy seeks the man responsible for the deaths of many men, including his younger brother. When the trail leads him to Bluestone Creek, his search for justice becomes entwined with the plight of local farmers and a rancher. Clancy's battle escalates when his meddling uncovers cattle theft, and endangers a young woman, her sister and father. The stakes are lethal and when the final battle comes, Clancy's trail of vengeance may cost all four of them their lives . . .